Like The Flies
On The Patio

ALSO BY NANCY KLANN-MOREN

The Clock Of Life

Like The Flies
On The Patio

STORIES

Nancy Klann-Moren

Anthony Ann Books

Versions of these stories have appeared elsewhere:
"The Lois and Clark Affair," in *Art Times*, June, 2009 and *She Writes Anthology*, 2011.
"The m&m's" also in the *She Writes Anthology*, 2011.
"The Silver Twinkie" in *A Year in Ink Anthology*, 2012 and *The Huffington Post* June 6, 2013
The story, "Fate Carries Its Own Clock," was the seed that sprouted into the novel, "The Clock of Life."

www.nancyklann-moren.com

Anthony Ann **Books**

ISBN: 978-0-9884944-2-8

For Sydney and Sebastian
and Kyah and Amira and Layla,
and for Richard, again

Contents

The m&m's

The Noisy Pelican is a seaside bar that serves tortillas and beans and three-buck lager until seven p.m. every night of the week. I go there to eat and haven't cooked since Louie walked out on me last year. My waistline has spread from too many of the tortillas, with a roll of fat that I reach for and grip nice and tight when I'm feeling lonesome.

Louie used to take me out for steaks with all the trimmings and say wonderful things to me. When he touched me, he said my skin felt like white velvet. He loved my red hair and would nestle his nose deep into it and then say he could smell the family we would make together. Anymore, when I sit home alone, I wonder whose hair he's smelling now—so I stay mostly at the bar.

Natalie would talk about Louie with me. She and I were best friends since the third grade, and talked about everything. We always said that life's a game, like *Wheel of Fortune*. Six months ago, on her thirty-second birthday, Natalie spun the wheel, landed on *lose your turn,* and was out of the game. She broke her leg while tripping on a curb and died when a blood clot shot to her heart—and mine.

We used to talk about having adventures. About saving our money and running away together to the South of France. We wanted to go topless and have French men admire us. We wanted them to look at us with a smoldering European desire and say things we couldn't understand. She died before I found out that the beach on the boardwalk in Nice is rocky and uncomfortable and that French men think they're too good for American girls, unless they're girls with a lot of money.

Natalie would have liked Dewalt's advice to me. I think she would have even liked Dewalt. One night he plopped down on the stool beside me. I usually sit on the third stool from the corner, and feel put-upon if strangers perch their butts on my spot. Dewalt said he drives a Zamboni. At first I thought it was a sports car until he said it was the machine that smoothes out the ice during hockey games.

His chest puffed up as he bragged about his hockey friends like they were movie stars or millionaires. The Big Dogs, he called them. Dewalt wasn't bad looking at all, with tousled blonde hair and playful eyes. His hands were small. I imagined it would take larger hands to drive one of those ice machines. Big hands wrapped in insulated gloves.

When he spoke, I watched his chunky mustache bounce, and I wondered how the Zamboni cleared away the blood from the ice. His lip curled when I asked about the blood. "Red Ice," was all he said.

He rolled up the sleeves of his flannel shirt and showed me jagged scars that he'd gotten from breaking up fights on the ice. A small tattoo on the upside of his right forearm looked homemade. The thin, uneven letters spelled, Dr. Smooth. My eyes traveled down to his small hands. Then, as if he'd known me forever, Dewalt offered to get me a free ticket to come to a game and see him work.

Despite myself, I started telling him about Louie leaving me. About how Louie wanted a son real bad, and no matter how much we tried, he called me lazy for not giving him one. Every night, when we'd go to bed I'd get a talking-to that felt like a scolding. The more he talked, the colder the fire inside me got, until it was nothing more than lifeless ashes. I'd close my eyes and want to turn my back to him, but I stayed until he was the one who left.

Dewalt got a knot between his eyebrows and listened like he knew how I felt. Then he moved his hand to my shoulder. It felt bigger than it looked. He said it was time for me to decide whether I was going to live my life as a stick or as a puck.

I sounded like a bleeding-heart and changed the subject from Louie to Natalie. I told Dewalt about the time we found a diary in a second-hand store that smelled like tomcats and old doilies full of dust and starch. It was a leather-bound book with a locking clasp and gold, fancy writing on the cover that said "A Line A Day."

A girl named Doris Hartman had written in it fifty years before we found it. We stretched out on the cement floor and read every page like Peeping Toms gawking through an old windowpane. The ink on the pages looked like thin, blue thread set free from its spool.

We found out Doris was a rich girl, and her dainty handwriting told of dancing parties and long-ago luxury liner trips.

February 8 – Saturday – Arrived in Hong Kong. Shopped on shore – Had dinner with Billie Pape, and Mr. Nelson joined us after dinner for dancing – a peach of a time – had 4 "cut-in's" – could only dance two. One was

*with Mr. Bates, much to Pape's distress. Oh!
How I love to dance.*

*March 30 – Monday – The peak of so much
change of climate came today. I fainted, falling
head first down the stone stairs of the Imperial
Hotel. Mr. Bolton carried me to my room, and
he dressed my wounds. It made me terribly
nervous, and I couldn't go to the Smith's for
lunch. I'm lonesome and disgusted with Tokyo. I
miss Jamie and regret I must start school in San
Andreas before my folks arrive.*

For me, reading the diary entries was like
crawling through an escape hatch. I wasn't sure if
Natalie felt the same, and I guess I didn't really care
because I bought the diary for her as a birthday
present. We decided it would be great fun to search
for the girl who wrote in the book. Maybe, just
maybe, she would still be alive. Louie didn't want
us to go, but when Natalie and I got something in
our minds, we were power.

Dewalt liked hearing about me and Natalie, and
bought me a beer. We touched mugs, and he said,
"Here's to Natalie. Ya miss her, don't ya?" I told
him life since she died is like breathing only
halfway in.

Natalie had the beauty of a proud animal. She
had strong bones covered with tight, umber-shaded

skin. She saw things through troubled puppy eyes, the color of tobacco, and said things through heavy lips. When we met on the handball court in third grade, I wanted to touch her skin that shined like a waxed dining table, and hold her hand that had big knuckles.

Our friendship was instant. It was comfortable, like high-top sneakers that are tied real loose. We were iron particles drawn into the same magnetic field, Natalie and me. She had a wonderful name. Natalie Dorotea Ontario Salamanca Martinez. I memorized it and liked to say it out loud. Both our last names started with M, Martinez and Mitchell, and we called ourselves the m&m's even after we both got married. Natalie twice, Garcia and Rivera. Me once, to Louie Chapman.

My tongue was loose, but Dewalt didn't seem to mind, so I talked about Louie some more. About how we met. About his yellow hair, thick like lamb's wool. He had a sweet, flat face, like a koala bear, with bulging eyes, and he talked nonstop. Louie sometimes sought support from an organization that helps people who hear a hum inside their heads but don't suffer from a hearing disorder.

We met at the Noisy Pelican on his first day in town. He stopped by after emptying a truckload of furniture at his new place down the street. Louie leaned towards me when he talked and tapped my arm gently to make a point. That very touch made me light-hearted and playful, and sexy and alive. He talked up a blue streak, and I threw my head back in laughter. I went to his apartment that night to help him set up his house, and I'm still there now.

After we got married, it upset him when Natalie and I still called ourselves the m&m's. He said I was a Chapman and didn't need to go back to my maiden initial, even for a nickname. But Natalie and I had been friends too long to be called anything else.

When we took the diary and headed out to find Doris Hartman, we stocked the car with giant bags of candy, both plain and peanut. We drove north, with the windows down, grabbing the wind with our hands. We were headed to Mill's College, near Oakland, where we knew from reading the diary, that Doris attended school.

Before she went off to college her mother had bought her a car. Doris named it Alexander the Great, but called it Alex.

> *August 11 – Monday – Oh! Oh! What a wonderful last few days these have been. Received a letter from dearest Dad – he's sending me a Diamond. I got word from the dressmaker that the formal is ready, and took a ride in Alex today.*

> *August 17 – Monday – Thrills! Thrills! I took my medical exam, completed registration, made out my program, and paid the tuition at Mills – all is well.*

Natalie seemed more interested in stopping at Gilroy than getting up to Mills. The signs along the road said, GILROY – The Garlic Capital of The World. She said Doris could wait—that I shouldn't make such a big deal.

I was anxious to move on but followed her as she took her sweet time strolling through the airless tourist shops with sawdust floors and cluttered shelves filled with garlic-shaped hats and refrigerator magnets.

She flirted with a clerk who recommended garlic as a remedy for headaches, bites, worms, tumors, heart ailments, and God knows what else. Natalie clasped her chin and nodded with interest like her head was loose. I watched her raven-black hair bounce, the way hair moves in shampoo commercials when he talked about the magical powers of garlic and how the Romans took it for strength during battles.

The whole town smelled like a belch. I went back to the car to wait, realizing that Natalie didn't care about Doris the way I did. Natalie made fun of her spoiled ways, but to me, she seemed very lonely. Her parents were never around, and I thought of Gloria Vanderbilt, the *Poor Little Rich*

Girl. I got a dull sinking feeling in my heart when reading some of the pages as if I could feel the long, dark night of her soul. As though she could feel mine, too.

> *October 21 – Wednesday – **My 22nd Birthday** – The girls came into my room with a box of Rocky-Road and helped me eat them.*

> *October 23 – Friday – Oh Dear! I'm sick of being a dumb-bell. Why can't I be like other girls and do things? Can I never overcome my self-consciousness? Is there nothing in me?*

Natalie didn't have the kind of ears that heard the pages crying out. She'd grown up in a neighborhood of field workers with no time for self-pity. Her family lived in a complex of World War II Quonset huts. Fourteen stood side by side, looking like giant loaves of steel bread lined up along the train track. For ten years, the Martinezs lived in the front half of the third building until they finally moved into a stucco house far from the trains.

When she read the diary, Natalie could only see the diamonds and cars, and dreamed of the beautiful crystal beads that Doris wore.

> *November 9 – Tuesday – Mother arrived home today with loads of pretty things. A dress*

& beautiful fur for me – also several strings of crystal beads.

We wondered what she looked like. Natalie thought of Rita Hayworth or Ann Blythe. I wanted her to look like Ingrid Bergman—the way she looked with Bogart in Casablanca. We talked about meeting her as an old woman.

Dewalt excused himself. I thought he'd gone to the john, but he came back with m&m's from the vending machine by the pay phone. He emptied the bag onto the counter between us and stared at my hair as he dragged each red one over to his side. The rest, he said, were for me. "Red is the color of the strength that pumps through our hearts," he said. "Ya know, your hair reminds me of a halo of strength."

Then, as if sort of embarrassed, he turned the conversation back to Doris by asking if we ever got to meet her. I told him about going into the library at Mills College. It was a quiet, empty place, except for the hum of the air conditioner and the taps of our flip-flops. We asked an overweight woman at the front counter where we could look up an old student. The woman wore a blue nametag that said, Miss Iggy.

"The historical annuals are stored downstairs," she said, with a suspicious stare. We gave her the years Doris was at Mills. "Have a seat at one of the tables. Only staff is allowed in the archives. I'll do my best."

Doris' picture was in three of the books. She looked straight at me with a numb smile. Her skin was as pale as mine, but her eyes seemed far away. Her bobbed hair was dark, with a side part. In all three photos, she wore a strand of crystal beads.

The hairs on my arms rose as footsteps shuffled past. I thought they could be Doris' and didn't look up for fear of disappointment. Time lingered as I looked past the pages into her fixed eyes. Doris had jewels and beautiful clothes, but she didn't have friends like I had Natalie.

We turned the pages in silence, looking for more. There was no more.

I read the diary out loud another time while Natalie drove back home down the coast. The words were like an echo that bounced back at me.

December 27 – Friday – Feelin kinda heavy and blue. What a year it has been. We never know from one minute to the next where we'll be.

We talked about our next trip, to San Andreas where Doris lived. Back then, we were on a journey to the past, but now I can't go back for the girl who wrote to us so long ago, without Natalie. Hell, I can't even get off the barstool.

I stopped talking and looked over to see that the red m&m's were gone. Dewalt's face turned serious. "Natalie might not have known what you felt, but I do."

I smiled for the first time in a year and told Dewalt I'd like to see him drive the Zamboni at the next hockey game.

The Silver Twinkie

It'd been three decades since I last saw Yvonne Carter, and never would I have made the drive if she hadn't needed me.

After five hours, the highway became less and less congested, until mine was the lone car on the isolated road. The Mojave Desert scenery stretched for miles and seemed unforgiving. Yucca and barrel cactus rippled through ponds of distant vapors like caution signs. The tour books call it desolate grandeur, but it seemed more like windswept insanity.

Yvonne and I had been best friends during the roller-skating years—the laugh-til-you-blow-milk-out-of-your-nose stretch from third grade until the second summer of middle school, when the Carters abruptly moved. We promised to stay close, but as those things go, we lost touch.

After the initial excitement of hearing from her, I asked how she had found me.

"On the internet," she said. "I use the library computers for free." Her voice hissed over a poor connection. "It was easy. I plunked in a couple of matter-of-facts, and I'll be damned if your name and address didn't come up on the screen."

"I'm so glad you did."

"Fancy schmancy you," she said. "Living in Beverly Hills."

"On the outskirts." I laughed. "How about you?"

"I'm in the desert," she said. "God, I've missed you over the years, Rosy."

"I've missed you, too," I said, uncomfortable with my fib.

"Whenever I'm feeling unhinged, I look at the photo of us at Magic Mountain, and somehow it helps me. Remember how much fun we had that day?"

"Well, sure," I said. But I didn't really. Not the way she did. She recited word-for-word details of conversations and then recounted other trips we'd taken—exact details about what we wore and how the mustard from the corn-dogs dripped down our arms. I grew self-conscious about my memory. It was as though a giant blotter expunged all the details of our friendship. Even so, some of the things she said simply couldn't have happened. Or maybe they could have.

Yvonne sounded a bit wacky, and, that part I remembered well. Soon, just like when we were kids, she made me laugh. We grew nostalgic over tap dance lessons, two-handed canasta games during summer break, and listening to the Top 40 Countdown together. Our conversation glided smooth as a waltz, with Yvonne taking the lead and filling in all the particulars.

"Remember how you'd bail me out of trouble?" she said. "How you could rationalize to the teachers until nothing we did was our fault?"

I was flattered. I think.

"Are you still loyal to the bone, Rosy? Still polite as punch? Still perfect as a china doll? Can you still talk your way out of anything?"

"Yvonne, stop it." Even though her voice remained airy, I feared the teasing could turn mean.

"Okay, Okay, but God, I'd love to see you again. I'd drive to your place in a heartbeat, but my car's on the blink."

"Is it serious?"

"I like to say it bit the dust."

"What?"

"Like I said, I'm out here in the desert, and somehow, sand from a dust storm got into the gas tank. I'll get it fixed when I can."

"I'm out there often," I said, assuming she meant Palm Springs.

"Great. Why don't you come see me next time you're here? I'm going to be off work for the next few weeks, so we can shoot for that."

"Off work?"

"I've got some bum joints. Surgery's scheduled for next week. They'll replace the knuckles on my right hand with plastic implants."

"I'm open the weekend after next. I can drive out for a visit and help you after the surgery. Two birds."

"That'd be swell."

"Why don't you e-mail me the directions?"

"I'll just tell them to you now."

The thing is, she didn't live in Palm Springs. When she said, "By Death Valley, near the Nevada border," I wanted to pull my words out of the phone wires and yank the offer back. The name alone, Death Valley, smacked of danger. I imagined scorpions, and vultures, and crusty-skinned men carrying long-barreled rifles for shooting at empty beer cans and rattlesnakes. It was much further than Palm Springs and the opposite direction to boot.

As each day passed, my regret of telling her I'd come to see her grew. An intuition, or foreboding, assisted by my normal stressed, neurotic self, convinced me we had nothing in common—that we never had.

Twice I picked up the phone to call with an excuse, but I didn't because hearing from her awakened a lightness in me that had been sleeping since my divorce.

My behavior was horrible during the split-up, and I felt out of touch with the world. Our friends sided with John. I thought a good deed might get my life back on track. Maybe I needed my old friend back. Or my childhood.

The thought of returning home was constant, but I drove on as if powered by the menacing heat. Part of me was anxious to reminisce. To laugh with abandon, like when we were two little girls who wanted to ride on lightning bolts and shake hands with astronauts. Another part of me felt trapped in a web of politeness and the inability to say no.

Wind gusts shook the car. A moth's wing flapped next to a yellow glob on the windshield. It reminded me of the insects Yvonne caught in elementary school from the windowsills above the stalls of the girls' bathroom. She'd rip one wing off and watch the creature thrash about the tiled floor, in circles.

Soon, bug debris was all over my brand-new Jaguar. The bleakness of the trip expanded with my anxiety. I reached for my cell phone to call Yvonne and beg off with an excuse. The signal was low, on its last bar. I scrolled through the menu for her number, just as the truck Yvonne described, came to view.

"You'll pass an old, rusty panel truck," she said. "Sittin' on concrete blocks. It's hard to miss. The word OOPS is spray painted across the side."

The letters were huge and sloppy, with drips streaking down to the running board. A knot settled in my stomach as I passed by.

"Keep driving," she said. "Seventeen miles past the truck, turn right and keep going straight until you see the Shady Cabana Trailer Estates." I stuck the phone back in its holster and scolded myself for the panic attack

When she told me she lived in a trailer park, I imagined one like my grandparents' old vacation home. The two-bedroom doublewide was perched on a lush cliff overlooking the Pacific Ocean. To enjoy the view, we sat on comfortable patio furniture under an aluminum awning.

Yvonne's runty trailer could have been abandoned if it weren't for the prickly-pear garden and two plastic flamingos perched next to the hitch. The cocoon-shaped Airstream was pocked with dents. It looked crippled, supported by cracked, airless tires. A homemade sign next to the filmy louvered windows read, "The Silver Twinkie."

The door opened. A woman filled the entrance. She had on a sleeveless muumuu, the same color as the blue painted on her puffy eyelids. I wasn't sure if it was Yvonne until she stepped into the garden and waved. Swollen skin covered the features of the girl I once knew.

I pulled onto the pebbled drive behind a faded red Ford Festiva and adjusted the rear-view mirror to check my face, hoping it would hid the dread inside my chest. If only I'd listened to my intuition.

Yvonne made her way to my car. The contrast in our size was extreme, and I wished I'd worn something less tailored.

When I stepped out of the Jag, we embraced. My cheek pressed against her damp muumuu, which smelled of sweat and mildew.

"Holy shit, Rosy, you look like a kid," she said, and stepped back. "I'll be damned. You haven't changed one bit."

"Yvonne, it's nice of you to say that. And look at you. Where did you get that dress? Periwinkle's one of my favorite colors. It complements your eyes."

"Periwinkle? Hell, I just thought it was blue. Hey, that's one damn pretty set of wheels you're driving. What is it?"

I nodded and forced a smile, wishing, for the first time, I didn't have such a nice car.

"Come on inside." She offered her hand. A straight, healthy hand, fingers tipped with bright coral polish, no bandages or signs of surgery.

"Welcome to my abode." Yvonne opened the door. It gave a husky whine. "This here's a 1962 Globetrotter. They're hard to find anymore," she said, with a tone of pride. "I bought it from a couple of tin-can tourists who traveled just for fun. But Twinkie hasn't gone anywhere since I've owned her."

When we stepped inside, the linoleum floor bounced as if attached to springs. The heavy smell of pork and beans filled the space. She closed the door tight. The swamp cooler droned. It seemed as if I could span the trailer from kitchen to sleeping area in five or six steps.

"Sit, sit, sit," she said like she was training a puppy. I obeyed by sitting on the tweed sofa behind a maple coffee table with an empty shoestring potato can on it.

Yvonne sat across from me on an upholstered bench next to a worn Formica table.

"How long have you lived here?"

"Twenty years," she said. "This kind of living's not for everyone, but after a while, it feels as comfortable as a mother's womb." Her words mixed with a laugh of short air blasts. "It's about the same size."

She reached into her pocket and pulled out a

pack of cigarettes, then stretched to grab an ashtray from the bookshelf next to her. An ice pick balanced on the top shelf. The words, Death Valley Ice Company, were stamped on the wooden handle in red block letters.

Instead of lighting up, she said, "My liver's startin' to rumble. You want to join us?"

"Us?"

"Usually, it's just me and Jack." She got up and looked toward the kitchen area. A bottle of Jack Daniel's sat on the counter by the sink. I checked my watch. It was close to two in the afternoon, and I hadn't been there five minutes. I don't drink before five.

"Sure," I said.

"Good."

The floor gave as she walked to the kitchen nook. The small, veneer cabinets above the sink were latched with oversized bobby pins fastened through eyehooks. Yvonne's muumuu filled the space. She poured us some Jack, no ice.

"Rosy, you see how easy things are when you live unpretentious?" Again, she laughed, noisy air mixing with her words.

Her manicured hands wrapped around the glasses. She set my drink on the coffee table and plopped back on her bench. The Silver Twinkie closed in like a cage.

"I thought you were having surgery," I said.

"What surgery are you talking about?" One of her eyes twitched a little. "Damn, it's good to see you, Rosy. Let's drink to Peachgrove Street and to the 'friends-forever' bracelets we made." Yvonne shoved her meaty, formless wrist toward me. "Remember how we made these from the catgut strings of that old tennis racket?" Her hand stayed put. "Remember how we'd share a roll of Lifesavers every Saturday and promised-on-spit that nothing would come between us?"

"Not really," I said. My head began to throb.

Her eye twitched again. "Well, that's real damn convenient, isn't it Rosy. I don't suppose you remember Skippy Howard either." Her voice slipped into a singsong, juvenile tone.

"Skippy Howard? Which one was he?"

"You stole him from me with your brand new la-de-da bike. Your fancy Christmas present, with the streamers on the handlebars."

I laughed. "Yvonne?"

"Not funny, Rosy," she snapped. "How about Roger Jennings and Stevie Hinkle and Bobby Farley? I don't suppose you remember them either. You, strutting around in your designer clothes and cashmere sweaters, going off to Cotillion with all the rich boys, while I stayed home."

"What's going on, Yvonne? Those were horrible boys. You were lucky you didn't have Cotillion." I looked toward the door. "I always envied you getting out of those affairs. I wanted to be you and not have to go to them."

"Yep, you're still Miss Twist-Things-Around."

The sickly sweet smell of the brown sugar bubbling in the pork and beans crawled up my nostrils. I thought, Jesus, how can I get out of here politely? I looked at the floor and saw brown spots on the linoleum. Perfectly round drips, like dried blood. Or it could have been sauce from the pork and beans.

"So, do you live here alone?" I said.

"Only since Larry died."

Our eyes met. My insides tightened. "Larry? Your husband?"

"Yep. Well, common law."

"That's okay."

"Larry was a loser. A real whack job." She took a sailor's gulp of Jack. "When we met, he drove a taxi. By the time we moved in together, he was a part-time drunk, a part-time bricklayer, and a full-time man of God."

"A man of God?"

"He was crazed with the Holy Scriptures." She shook her head. "His own damn version. He wasn't Baptist or Presbyterian or anything like that. He was a self-serving Man Of God with a Dodge Ram pulpit."

She put her hands in the air. Her voice dropped. "Praise be, God in heaven," she said. "Help my wife accept her journey of penance. Hold her hand as she walks through this life of purgatory. Lord Jesus, make her understand." Her speech pattern changed, as though she was channeling Larry and mocking him at the same time. "Let her know you intend her no harm, even though she is reminded every day because she lives with the devil's stupidity."

Yvonne leaned forward and coughed. White spittle collected in the corners of her mouth. I noticed movement past her shoulder on the bookshelf. A roach crawled over the ice pick.

"He was an unpredictable freak, Rosy. I never knew what to expect next." She took another drink. "Every week brought seven days of damnation for the unclean spirits that dwell in us all. Myself, in particular."

"Wow." I didn't know what else to say.

"He was a goddamn madman, Rosy."

Yvonne watched me reach for my purse and set it on my lap. My keys had been on top but slipped inside with the sudden movement.

"Goodness, what happened to him?" I tried to ask casually, but the words came out shaky.

"I was on the front steps watching him preach to no one from his truck bed. The Dodge rocked from his gyrations like it'd been caught in its own little earthquake. He squealed about brimstone and the fire that never shall be quenched." Yvonne's face began to pinch.

I wanted to scream at the top of my lungs and bolt out the door right then, but was afraid it was locked. My hand searched deep in my purse. The keys were nowhere.

"His face was gray as ash, and his arms were stretched out, fingers shaking like a son-of-a-bitch." She stood up to show me, and the Silver Twinkie moved.

"He was shouting to the Holy Ghost, and the veins in his neck jumped like they were trying to escape. One big fat vein finally burst, and Larry fell flat. He choked on his own sermon."

I froze because of the way she stared at me.

What did you do?" I asked quickly.

"I made a joyful noise unto the Lord, Rosy. He'd finally given me a sign."

"Praise the Lord, Yvonne." I don't know why I said that, but then I added, "I guess God's looking out for you."

"You betcha, Rosy. And every day, I thank him for taking Larry away." She smiled like it was a perfectly normal thing to say. "And now he's sent you back to me." She brought her hands together and rubbed them in a menacing gesture.

"Let's celebrate. More Jack?"

Without my answer, Yvonne took the ice pick from the bookshelf and went to the kitchen. But, Yvonne hadn't put ice in our first drinks.

"No more for me, thank you." I looked down at the brown dots on the floor, again convinced they were blood.

"Everything's just fine now," she said gently. "Now that I have you here."

I got up and ran to the door. It didn't budge. Yvonne turned.

"What are you doing, Rosy?"

Our eyes met. Her pupils looked microscopic inside the blue, puffed lids. She reached for my arm with a clammy hand. I breathed in her stench.

"You don't need to go anywhere, Rosy. Sit back down and visit awhile."

I stayed where I was. "For God's sake, Yvonne, you said you were having surgery. I came here to help you. I'm just here to help."

"I don't need no surgery." She smiled. "I said that to get you to come out. Don't you know, Rosy, I wanted to see you so bad. I didn't think you'd come unless I fibbed just a little. Hell, you're the one who taught me how to do that—fib just a little."

I jerked my arm from her soggy clutch. Yvonne stepped back. I thought I saw the ice pick in her far hand—the hand with the catgut bracelet.

The surge of fear hit me as hard as if the ice pick had struck my temple. I screamed at the big blue monster that smelled bad, and punched my right fist deep into her enormous, gummy belly. My hand hit a pillow of fat, and then the hard sack of intestines met my knuckles.

Yvonne fell back. Her head smacked on the corner of the bookshelf. Her menacing eyes turned empty. She slid to the floor. I moved the excess material of her muumuu with my shoe, to look for the pick, but only saw the dried blood drips, and nothing else. The low-pitched growl of the swamp cooler turned haunting.

Yvonne tried to get up and then fell back. When I charged toward the door, I saw the Death Valley Ice Company pick still on the counter next to our glasses.

The door wasn't locked, just stuck. After two shoves, it scrapped against the threshold and opened.

Once free from the Twinkie, I ran. The bite of a barrel cactus ripped through the leg of my pants and caught some skin. While stumbling toward the car, I dug into my purse for the keys. They rattled, a maddening sound, but I couldn't feel them. My hand dug deeper through tissues, half used matchbooks, and plastic toothpicks. I set the bag on the hood, looked back toward the Twinkie to make sure Yvonne was still inside, and frantically turned the bag upside down.

My wallet tumbled out. Credit cards and loose change slid under the car. Then, everything else in the purse cascaded to the ground. The beautiful, life-saving Jaguar emblem on my keychain peeked out from a tear in the lining.

A throaty moan seeped from the Twinkie. The trailer swayed. Yvonne stumbled outside to the top step.

"Rosy," she called. "What are you doing? Please don't go. Please don't be mad at me."

"Get away from me," I screamed as I got into my car. "Get away, you sick, deceitful cow."

"Please don't go, Rosy, please don't be mad at me!"

The key turned but stopped with the flat click of a faulty starter. It clicked and clicked, then nothing. Yvonne came down the steps. I locked the car and turned the key again. She reached for my door handle.

One last panic-filled try, and the engine whirled in a triumphant roar. I put the gearshift in reverse. My foot shoved the pedal to the floorboard, and the Jag roared backward.

Gravel battered the underside of the car as I sped to the highway, with the moth wing still flapping on the windshield. The wind had died down and the world seemed to slow to a more normal pace. I rolled down the windows. The desert air dried my moist eyes as I accelerated past the panel truck on cement blocks with the word spray painted on the side. OOPS.

The Lois and Clark Affair

Her husband was out of town on a business trip, and rather than drive home to an empty house after work, she went to Prima Pasta, one of the many bistros that dotted the coast highway. A typical spot, where straw-covered Chianti bottles sat on the tables and paintings from local artists covered the walls.

She didn't go there to eat, but enjoyed the magnetic scent of garlic and herbs that followed her into the bar next to the dining room. After she positioned herself on the barstool, the man to her left began speaking to her. His head bobbed, and his words came out in high-pitched chirps. A thick accent made him difficult to understand. Still, she gathered his mother had been a frail woman and recently fallen quite ill. She half-listened out of politeness, but her eyes turned away when she'd had enough of his gloomy conversation.

A man with an easy, open smile caught her attention. His boyish face triumphed over his grey-flecked hair and creases that ran from his nose to the outside of his full lips. He wore a yellow cardigan, tortoiseshell glasses, and a wedding band. The empty stool to her right separated them.

She watched him talk with a bearded man in a blue and white seersucker suit, who puffed on a plastic cigarette with an LED light on the tip. It glowed with each inhale. The appealing man glanced toward her several times. With an ambushed expression, he said, "You've got to help me. May I move over next to you?"

"Please, yes. I could use a little help myself."

They collided, bumping heads as he shifted to move over.

"My name's Clark."

Her dark hair fell forward and covered her lean face as she reached to shake his hand. "Clark, you're not going to believe this, but my name is Lois. Did you come here to save me?" She instantly wished those lame-brained words hadn't escaped from her mouth.

"Maybe we saved each other."

He was the first man named Clark she had ever met, and it seemed like an invitation to something exclusive. Lois Lane had been much more than a fictional character to her when she was young. She had been, well, real. Every time she saw a *Superman* rerun on the family television, she watched Clark Kent save and protect Lois. Unconditionally.

Her affinity toward Lois Lane was dreamy and had to do with her—*their* destinies and their names. Just like the leading lady on the weekly T.V. show, she had always felt the perfect man for her—her prince, shining knight, and hero—would be named Clark.

Over twenty years later, in the instant it took him to say his name, she was seized with expectation. He hailed from Kansas, chatted about a recent rafting trip down the Colorado River, and ordered Bombay Sapphire gin. He liked to play golf as often as possible and didn't like the government requiring him to fasten his seat belt.

She smelled a distant hint of juniper when he put his hand on her arm. His firm touch felt warm on her skin. It reached deep into her nerve endings, causing them to dance with anticipation, as if emerging from a fallout shelter after years of isolation.

She felt her mood climb in the direction of the

future, like a seed sprouting toward an artificial stimulus. A buoyant part of her broke free in animated gestures and deep, throaty laughs. Her cheeks became ruddy. She was a carnal desert in need of a heavy rain.

Lois didn't talk about her profession, colleagues, or research projects, and her husband wasn't mentioned. Instead, she told Clark some of the soft things about herself: about her love of modern art and ballet, and how when crossing bridges she still believed there might be a troll lurking underneath.

She described her favorite beach, complete with sandpipers dancing with the tides. Clark said he liked the way her eyes greeted laughter willingly and that her whole face smiled when she talked. Then he checked his watch.

"Have you had dinner?"

"I had a late lunch. I guess I'm drinking my dinner."

"Please, keep me company. Let's get a table and have something to eat."

The small table was far from the kitchen noise, near a corner fireplace. A neglected log had burned out, but it still carried the scent of smoldering intimacy. Their surroundings narrowed to the confines of two, and somehow, very quickly, narrowed more. Her head pulsed to the rhythm of her fantasy. She called forth imaginary characters from the city of Metropolis and placed them at the table.

They talked about music and favorite cities. They decided, together, that croutons and strawberries were overrated because you have to eat too many to find a good one. She became flush from her reverie and absorbed with the idea of Lois and Clark, fate and magic, and being taken care of forever.

Busboys cleared the surrounding tables as she talked once more about her favorite beach.

"Why don't we get out of here and go there together?" he said.

"That sounds great."

There they were, wrapped in a surreal mist, walking barefoot in a sheltered cove not far from the restaurant. She had walked along that shore often in daylight, but the night sky stretched the dark cliffs and amplified the sound of the waves. that pounded with urgency.

With the first kiss, the surf ran carelessly over their feet and rushed up their legs without warning. Then it fled back to the ocean and played with undercurrents of desire and illusion. Lois and Clark stayed there, saturated in themselves, for hours.

In Clark's hotel room, with its artificial plants and reproduced artwork, she felt strangely safe, the way it feels when looking at faded photographs of unknown relatives. She could have been in a fortress like the ones in make-believe stories.

She paid for their night together with pocketfuls of denial and made love between sips of champagne in a blue-stemmed glass. He touched her with whispers. She listened and permitted herself to savor her recklessness.

With an innocent stroke of his hand, the stone on Clark's wedding ring caught the locket that hung from her neck, an anniversary gift with her husband's picture inside. The chain ripped the smooth flesh of her neck.

She lay there, startled in an aroused emptiness. Darkness hid the blood that congealed on her neck and heightened the irony of their separate declarations of fidelity.

Feeling fragile and restless on a bed turned coarse and soiled, she imagined a scar forming on her neck. A scar that would require concealer.

When dawn broke through the opening between the hotel drapes, she turned on her side and stared at his back. A galaxy of freckles, dark moles, and secrets appeared before her, looking like a human dot-to-dot puzzle with no numbers to help make sense of it.

The private world of her fantasy had vanished, with no eyewitnesses, no police reports, and no clause for that kind of casualty on any of her insurance policies.

He turned over and sleepily said, "Last night was wonderful."

She reached up past the locket and stroked her neck. She thought about Kryptonite and desire and laughed at herself for confusing Clark with Superman.

Like The Flies On The Patio

Part One

A Summer Without Spirit

The humidity's as thick and rank as the summer can give, and my skirt's hiked so far up my legs I'm stuck to the molded plastic chair. This bacon and tomato sandwich is pitiful. They're out of lettuce. A small joint like this gets the last of the deliveries, and with the breezeless, sweltering summer air, there are none—deliveries, that is.

And it's curious there aren't any flies on the patio. The drooping, half-decayed canopy smells of rotting palm fronds, and it's prone to flies hovering. They usually scurry about and then land on the yellow oilcloth table cover. *Shoo fly, humble pie, hover under God's blue sky.*

This patio space out front of the "Island Grill" was Hazel's attempt to create a tropical atmosphere right here in the middle of Missouri.

Hazel's been buried three years now, taken by cancer, and she left Buford behind to suffer from chronic broken heart disease. His finest brown shoes crunch up the gravel path when he visits her in the sacred soil every Sunday. That's the only day he's not in the kitchen wiping his fleshy hands against a food-stained apron and growling at the hired help to keep the coffee mugs filled.

The coffee's bad today, served up in this murky, wilted air, with cream chunks moving through it like slow-moving algae on a toxic lake. It's the weather. The slow deliveries, slow refrigeration, and slow service. *Dead cream, daydream, try to raise your self-esteem.* Stirring the coffee with the red and white plastic stick, is supposed to work the lumps into smaller pieces. But today, it only rearranges them—besides, stirring's too much work for someone as tired as I am.

Last night, in my bed, there was a flea. A big, fat, hungry flea. And me, I was the meal. An ankle for starters, and then a portion of left thigh. He moved up for a serving of extra tender arm flesh just inches below my pit. It seems it was so tasty that he took seconds. *Fat flea, eating me, Eddie's now a scarcity.*

And all I can think about is how that rat Eddie left me.

"Eddie," I said. "What's wrong?"

"If you don't know, you're an idiot," he said, then, quiet as Marcel Marceau, packed up his duffle and walked out.

It seems I knew him for forever. I thought he was my best friend, but he must have needed to get away from all this nothing more than he needed to stay with me. It's been close to a week since I watched the back of his car spit dark puffs of smoke and heard one piercing backfire as he drove off.

"Eddie, please don't leave," I yelled and ran halfway down the drive. Then, because my chest ached so much, I stopped and looked down to see if there was blood on my blouse.

I haven't done much since he left, except hang out on the patio. And my bed has been empty, save the flea, ever since. It's sad to sleep next to the emptiness that begs me to move there.

Today, there's a barefoot man here. I've seen him before. Same as then, his clay-colored waistline seeps out from a too-small tee shirt, and his feet hang down from the bottom rung of the stool.

Staring at his big-as-shoebox feet, with ten tootsie roll chunk toes, it rolls over and over in my mind. *Chunk, chunk, chipmunk, down so long his heart has sunk.*

These rhyme flits twiddle inside my head all the time. They buzz around just like the flies on the patio. *Rhyme flit, lickety-split, take a thought and make it fit.* I have many—rhyme flits, that is.

Both of us, the shoeless man and me, watch a tourist couple over by the pretend palm trees Hazel bought from a going-out-of-business sale at the One Stop Party Shop. The lady's posing for a picture and the husband's working the Olympus Smart-Plus camera with the concentration of a towboat captain pushing a barge up the Mississippi. *Click, click, double quick, this is not my bailiwick.*

It hurts my tired eyes to see his ketchup-red skin, the guy with the camera, all blistered from the weather of several days ago. Those days before this steamy moisture, when the sun grew so strong its heat moved up my nostrils and scorched the hairs inside with each inhale and scorched my spirit as well. Then, of course, Eddie left.

I don't feel like doing Jack today except sit and sweat and watch nothing go by, save the tourist couple. And it's curious about the flies not being here to share my coffee or scurry around the goop on the stick and the puddles that collect when there's a spill.

Besides, if I go home, I'll just watch Minnie Pearl on Hee Haw reruns. When I see Minnie Pearl, I think of when Hazel was here serving up smiles in her print aprons and brimmed hat fashioned from dandelion weeds. I remember the tap-tap of the sawed-off hammer she used on the butternuts to free the meat. Then she'd pass them around.

And I remember how she played Cribbage with her best friend, my mom. One of them would catch a case of the giggles, and straight away the other would join in. The two of them together sounded like bubbles of pure joy.

My folks are buried just a couple rows from Hazel, up there at Tucker's bone yard. *Real dead, newlywed, don't sleep in a double bed.* My folks got there first. Sometimes, it seems they've been there since time began.

They went together in Ol' Blue on their way to the Lake of the Ozarks. Like Grace Kelly, they plunged off the side of the road with no explanations or goodbyes.

My dad loved that Ol' Blue. I was only ten and never would have said it in front of him, but Ol' Blue was a rattletrap of a station wagon. A big, steely blue 1961 Ford Fairlane wagon with mileage registered across the odometer for the second time. Rusty and decrepit, that car sputtered, shimmied, wheezed and as it turned out, didn't want to die alone.

Dad was big. Plain-looking big, in overalls and his "Big Red Machine" ball cap. He didn't follow baseball, and I never learned why he always wore that hat.

It's not that he didn't like people, but it was clear he didn't like to *talk* to people. But, boy-oh-boy, he sure did talk to the radio. Despite his size, I remember how dainty he turned from one newscast to another while he muttered and cursed at the announcers.

Mom was the opposite of him—small and friendly. She read *Movie Star News* from cover to cover and then again. She couldn't get enough of that stuff.

The tourists just moved to the bench between the life-sized, coin-operated hula dancer and the wooden camel named Joe. He's a dromedary, I think. *Joe, Joe, mistletoe, tell me everything you know.* They ordered two Slo-Gin-Fizzes from Buford.

I know it disturbs him to see me sit around on the patio, doing little more than sulking, doodling, and jotting my rhyme flits on a napkin. And sometimes swatting flies.

Nothing Happens At The Island Grill

Shoo fly, humble pie,
hover under God's Blue Sky.
Nothing happens, days go by.

Dead cream, daydream,
try to raise your self-esteem.
Not today, just let me scream.

Fat flea, eating me,
Eddie's now a scarcity.
He left behind the warranty.

Rhyme flit, lickety-split,
take a thought and make it fit.
If you can't, give up and quit.

Real dead, newlywed,
don't sleep in a double bed.
Or a coffin, my worst dread.

Joe, Joe, mistletoe,
tell me everything you know.
Never mind, I gotta go.

Part Two

Creaking In The New Fall Air

No more than thirty seconds after I open the squeaky gate and plop down, Buford's daughter, Sophie, rushes up to help me. It's peculiar because she never rushes. But this morning she's here, lickity-split, to take my order; coffee and a short stack.

On weekends, Buford has her waiting tables to get her out of the kitchen, leaving him alone with his moods that explode like fireworks and his thoughts that make every day the fourth of July.

Sophie's thick hands cradle the coffee mug as she brings it to my table and sets it down with a clumsy thud. Then she uses those same big hands to delicately fuss over the chrysanthemum buds sticking out of the Pepsi bottle vase in the middle of the table, the same as her mama, Hazel used to.

That sends me off on a trip down memory lane, and I can't help but remember back to the past summer, before Eddie left, when he used to pluck flowers from the front yards as we walked passed on our way here to the Island Grill, and he'd gently stick them in my hair, above my ear.

But just as my heart starts to turn heavy from thinking about Eddie, that stray dog, the scrawny little Chihuahua excuse for a canine that Sophie insists on feeding, jumps on my right ankle and starts panting and drooling and humping and bumping. The twisted, bug-eyed freak gets-off by romancing another species' leg. God, he's annoying. I most certainly didn't invite him, so I poured the water from the Pepsi vase on him. *Pepsi vase, mouse face, dogs and legs should not embrace.* Poor mutt, wet and dejected, and all the same, still stays chock full of hope.

Then I notice the air smells of burnt leaves smoldering in heaps on the edge of town. Dried-out pods click and crackle along the sidewalk in the breeze. It's the very same breeze that shakes the leaves from the trees and throws them to the ground. There's no stopping them from falling. Every time a leaf falls, I remember something and miss it. *Fall air, teddy bear, wish I was a millionaire.* And I wish I'd stop missing things, and people.

Sophie looks like a million bucks today. I heard she met someone named Jackson Lee at the Turn-Around Dance last weekend over in Pulaski County. I don't dare bring it up, private and proud as she is, and don't have to because it shows through her skin, and her step, and her great big moony smile.

Sometimes, I think it's hard for Buford to look into Sophie's simple green eyes, the same color as his wife's. It must make him miss Hazel even more, like I miss Eddie.

And I miss his old Karman Gia with its limp,

good for nothing except putting it down, cloth top. *Rag top, flippity-flop, driving past the candy shop.* Running errands in a convertible feels like getting away with something — something secret. It, driving in a convertible, is like being handpicked by the sun and wind to sing with them, and share dance steps that swirl around and touch and touch again. Yes, it's days like this that I miss his noisy, whining, crippled car. And I miss him calling me Laurel and me calling him Hardy-har-har, and watching them, Laurel and Hardy, on the TV.

I remember before he left, he looked over at me with those crow-black eyes and told me I'm not exactly the life of the party. I told him he was the life of mine. And that's the way it was with him: ne loving him with all my heart, and all my heart not being enough. *Crow-black, heart attack, left behind your gunnysack.*

Today, I'm going to make a plan to move on.

One. Get out of this three-month "Eddie left me," pity party.

Two. Don't talk about Eddie or give him another thought.

Three. Develop a plan of action for a future without Eddie.

Four. Make sure Eddie's things. . .

Sophie just messed up my thought process by bringing me the butter-stained short stack smothered in syrup. We both watch Buford as he puts a quarter into the hula dancer's mouth. Hazel never gave her a name, but I call her Rita because I haven't ever met anyone with that name. The quarter passes through her lips, and Rita's hips and arms move in little jerks. They pick up speed at the very moment a flock of birds fly over the patio, migrating to Buenos Aries or somewhere else. And they honk their appreciation for her.

Hazel got Rita from a carnival that went bust. After all these years and all the quarters that have passed through her lips, today it sounds like her bones are creaking in the new fall chill, but she's still smiling. A faded smile. Nothing that touch-up paint can't fix—same as me.

Sophie likes to watch the hula dancer even more than I do. Buford brushes the quarters he feeds Rita with Hazel's leftover cherry-red nail polish to separate them from the tourist change. He wouldn't bother except for the very reason it makes Sophie so happy. *Sophie, chick-a-dee, solid as last year's trophy.* Before they died, my folks liked to see us kids happy, too.

Once, they won a golden trophy for a waltz contest at the Legionnaires' annual dance. A big gold ball with two dancers on top. First place. It's funny how the three of us, their very own children, never once saw them dance. And that beautiful trophy is the only proof they did. *Last dance, vest and pants, should have seen the kids advance.*

Sweet Lily, little Jack and me, our faces flush with pride, made a special place for it between the drawback curtains in the front window of the trailer. Every day, riding back from school on our bikes, we could see that trophy from the 'Show Me Home' Trailer Park entrance.

I loved that trophy and used to sing into it like it was a microphone. My sweet-tempered mom cried when I did that. The tears ran down her pale, thin face past the little red veins on her cheeks. Sometimes, they'd tumble down on her dress, but I'd keep right on singing.

And she got weepy when she read Old Mother Goose to us. "Then **Jack** went a-courting – A lady so gay – As fair as a **Lily** – And sweet as the **May.**" She read that one over and over, loudly punctuating our three names, and when she did this, she looked at us instead of the pages. *Dewy eye, don't die, sing a song of days gone bye.*

I still, to this day, have that dancing trophy tucked away in the cedar chest of memories and grief.

No one asked him to, but over the years, Buford's taken it upon himself to keep an eye on me. He watches me doodle my rhyme flits on the napkins and knows I take them home to keep with the others—napkins, that is. And he doesn't say it, but you can see in his eyes that he's glad Eddie has moved on.

Need Something Different At The Island Grill

Pepsi vase, mouse face,
dogs and legs should not embrace.
Go away, you're out of place.

Fall air, teddy bear,
wish I was a millionaire,
But I'm not, to my despair.

Rag top, flippity-flop,
driving past the candy shop.
Miss you, miss you. Have to stop.

Crow black – heart attack,
left behind your gunnysack.
Eever are you coming back?

Sophie, Chick-a-dee,
solid as last year's trophy.
Happy face, but so clumsy.

Last dance, vest and pants,
should have seen the kids advance.
Didn't happen – not a chance.

Dewy eye, don't die,
sing a song of days gone bye.
Think I'll order apple pie.

Part Three

My Heart Sang Old Winter's Sad Song

Sitting on the patio this time of year is odd. The winter sky meets the sidewalk and smothers the entire town with its boring tone. I think the patio's tropical setting and the smattering of Christmas lights strung above the tables was Hazel's attempt to battle the grayness.

This morning, I have a flask of brandy in my pocket. When I order my coffee black, Buford knows what I'm up to. He knows these things like a gypsy knows tarot cards.

"Good Morning, May," he says and dashes off so I can add the brandy without shame. He lets me sit alone behind puffy eyes covered with dark, movie-star glasses. *Movie star, so bizarre, puffy eyes won't get you far.*

The patio's cold, but I don't care Jack about that. Today I'd rather be outside watching my breath cloud than be inside.

Last night, my heart sang old winter's sad song. It hurt as much as if a jagged icicle had slit it. Sometime around ten o'clock, while alone in my bed, without Eddie for so very long, I inhaled the memory of his cologne. My passion for him turned into a winter fever. It festered and promised to erupt through a snowball that covered my heart. I cried frozen, brittle tears for myself and for all the times people have left me without a hug, a kiss, or a goodbye. And I cried because I couldn't stick to my plan about forgetting Eddie.

When I finally got to sleep, I dreamt of a little girl dog, Labrador I think, yelping and sitting up on her hind legs. She asked for a pat. Begging for nothing more than a pat. The pilot light went out, and I woke up shivering before I could reach out to her. Last night snaps back on me like a screen door, with a bang. I was the little dog.

The brandy's doing its business, and I want more. *More, more, matador, red cape, brandy, liquor store.* I can hear a conversation running through the phone wires lining the ally out back, and I wonder if feeling this sorry for myself is the first step to crazy. Sure as hell, I hear voices through the twisted cables, but can't make out what they're saying.

It's just like when I read the official clearinghouse sweepstakes announcements that come in the mailbox. I always think they've told me I won. But somehow, I get it wrong.

I keep all of them anyway, in a brown envelope that opens like an accordion and shuts with a string wound around a paper button. I save them with the hope that one day, when I'm nicely dressed, with clean hair and shiny lipstick, I'll look out my front window to see the prize patrol march up the three steps to my door, with a briefcase full of money.

Bankroll, prize patrol, come into my cubbyhole.

Then I'll go find Eddie and buy him back. But first, I'll take Aunt Gloria, sweet Lily, Jack and me to New York City.

Aunt Gloria was looking after us kids when Mom, Dad, and Ol' Blue took their fatal plunge. She was beautiful. Clear lake beautiful. She lived five spaces down from us in a yellow trailer called Lucy because of a really old movie where Lucy and Desi take a long, long trailer out west, or somewhere.

Back then, before we got word of the accident, Aunt Gloria had a wild streak. *Accident, lives were bent, didn't need abandonment.* But after that deadly day, she left Lucy, lived in our place, and took care of us until we, all three of us, went off to find our own accidents.

Nowadays, she's back living in Lucy. She watches old movies and dreams about one day seeing New York City. And she love, loves, loves, that's how she says it, Liza Minnelli.

Eddie's old friend, Michael Slay, went to New York once. Today, he's here on the patio, all hunched over, playing his mouth harp. Buford plunks a red quarter into Rita, and she's swaying to the bluesy, sweet suckling sounds coming from the harmonica. *Blues song, dance along, feelin like I don't belong.* It sounds good. I don't know whether to thank the brandy or something else. I want more blues and brandy, save the coffee.

It's been a while since anyone in town talked about Eddie around me. Everyone hushes up about him. It's best because when it comes to him, I can't talk. Hell, I can hardly breathe.

"It's time to stop about Eddie," I yell toward Michael Slay. "Way past time."

And while my words work their way across the space, it hits me as quick as flash bulbs shock eye sockets, that I was the one who stopped hugging.

Michael isn't paying any attention to me talking to no one, and that's okay, because sure as a nicotine patch helps you get over cigarettes, I realize I had stopped hugging first.

That very idea brings to mind how Eddie used to mope around, droopy-eyed and grouchy, and walk out of the room to start a conversation. He expected me to chase after the words and fetch whatever they requested. I remember growing weary of his bellyaching and tantrums. And when my spirits were flat as the pavement, he'd lower them further by calling me lame-brained.

Folks around here must have known I'd finally figure out for myself he was nothing but a lout. *Eddie lout, pig snout, took six months to sort it out.*

My flask's empty, but I'm still thirsty for something.

Seeing It Different At The Island Grill

Movie star, so bizarre,
puffy eyes won't get you far.
What's your preference at the bar?

More, more matador,
red cape, brandy, liquor store.
Winter's fever – what's life for?

Bankroll, prize patrol,
come into my cubbyhole.
Help me out, I need control.

Accident, lives were bent,
didn't need abandonment.
Time to change, and feel content.

Blues song, dance along,
feeling like I don't belong.
Stand up now and prove them wrong.

Eddie lout, pig's snout,
took six months to sort it out.
On my way with no more doubt.

Part Four

Spring Forward

Yesterday while visiting my folks up at the cemetery, I had the surprise of my life. In that world of stone slabs, holding a fist full of daffodils, I trotted like a pony past a cloud of darting bees, over to where Mom and Dad are buried.

"Hello," I said, then told them how much we all miss them. I tattered on about something of no great shakes when Mom interrupted me by singing.

"And when it's time for planting."

At first, I wasn't sure I'd heard it.

"I watch for signs of spring."

A song from Winnie the Pooh. I held my breath and didn't move.

"For budding seeds, or sprouting weeds, and the bounty they will bring."

I didn't look around to see if anyone was close by who could see me going insane up there on hallowed grounds.

Then she said, *"My sweet Mayflower,"* in the same voice I remember she used while reading to us when we were young.

"An introduction is to introduce people, but Christopher Robin and his friends, who have already been introduced to you, are now going to say goodbye."

I stood, for I don't know how long, frozen as the

gravestones in front of me. Then I said goodbye back.

I staggered down the gravel hill into town like there were ball bearings under my shoes, hearing her words in the pebbles beneath my feet. And all the while feeling hot and light and excited that I finally got to hear my goodbye. *Bye, bye, lullaby, thought my mom was close, nearby.*

Mom always said that the first time she saw me, I looked pretty as a May flower, and that's why she named me May. Little Jack was named after Dad. Lily and I are the only two who call him "little Jack" anymore—the only two who dare, him being six feet three inches tall.

He takes after Dad, big and quiet, and Mom, sweet and tender. Little Jack has a habit of filling his overall pockets with pistachio nuts. He cracks them open with his teeth and drops the empty shells to the ground. And he picks the nuggets from between his teeth with the corner of a matchbook. *Jack, Jack, quarterback, pick your teeth, then make a smack.*

I haven't told little Jack about visiting the folks up at Tucker's bone yard yesterday, but I told Lily. After the day I had, I couldn't help it.

Then, wouldn't you know, with all the excitement, insomnia set in last night, so I pulled out the old Smith-Corona to type some of the rhyme flits scribbled on the napkins lying around my place. They aren't coming to me as often as they did last summer—buzzing furiously. They've slowed some. I can think better.

The typewriter keys were stiff from years of sleep and piles of dust, but I managed to get them all typed and organized. Someday, maybe, I'll send the best ones off to the *Missouri Digest* for publication. *Rhyme flit, will submit, hope they think I have some wit.*

This morning, while walking to the patio in the fresh-as-tonic air, I feel a flicker of hope and promise. And it was nothing less than a miracle to get here and find out Buford has a new coffee machine, a Cory. It makes four pots at a time. It couldn't be better—the coffee, that is.

Wouldn't you know, Sweet Lily just breezes in looking like a paint ad, in a lavender dress, and periwinkle eye shadow.

"Hello, May," she says, as if it's a coincidence to see me. I know she's only here to check on me, to see if I look bonkers, and to make sure Buford hasn't noticed anything unusual. She's concerned about what the folks in town think, but I don't care Jack.

I shouldn't have called her when I got back home yesterday, babbling on like a full brook when the snow melts and sounding crazy enough to hear Mom read from *The House At Pooh Corner*, like when we were kids. I couldn't stop telling her what happened, over and over and again.

She made me promise I wouldn't breathe another word about it to anyone. Not even Aunt Gloria. I promised, but I had my fingers crossed because, damn it, I heard Mom say goodbye. I know what I heard. They, both Mom and Dad, knew how much I needed that, and now my heart has broken free from the battleship anchor that was keeping it down. *Battleship, round trip, pull up anchor, I won't flip.*

Sophie and Jackson Lee are out front having their picture taken before heading out of town on their honeymoon. Sophie, happiness coming out of her mouth and landing on her chin, reminds everyone that the clocks need changing tonight. She giggles and says she's winding hers back before she and Jackson Lee go to bed for an extra hour together. I think that's wrong—spring forward—but just nod and look into her simple green eyes, with envy.

Holy shit, my life just stopped fast as a motion picture when the film breaks. Eddie's on the other side of the bamboo gate.

He hops over and says, "May," as if it's hello. I haven't seen him since he drove off, the better part of a year ago. I'm flush with nerves and can't look away as he drops a quarter in Rita's mouth and plops himself in the chair across from me. His black eyes, beady like a rat's, squint as he gives me a half smile. His sharp chin spikes the air, and now he looks past me.

For one second, I want to hold his hand and tell him what Mom said to me, but I realize that the space between us is as solid as a firewall. *Firewall, ten feet tall, say goodbye, forget it all.*

I know that any minute now, I'll pick up the napkin I've been writing on and walk out the front gate, without a goodbye.

Hope and Promise At The Island Grill

Sopie Lee, tweedle-dee,
She and Jackson sure agree.
Hope and promise – thoroughly.

Bye, Bye lullaby,
thought my mom was close, nearby.
Sweet May, there's no need to cry.

Battleship, round trip,
Pull us anchor, I won't flip.
From now on, a pleasure trip.

Fire wall, ten feet tall,
Say goodbye – forget it all.
He's a jerk. I'll walk out tall.

Marcella's Martinis

Tired from all that goes with moving, I stopped unpacking and glanced out the window to watch snow flurries dance on pockets of air.

I threw on my quilted jacket, the closest thing to a winter coat I owned, and dragged the collapsed cardboard boxes down the back stairs to the dumpster in the alley.

Luminous flakes teased, reminding me of the time my mom described snowfall to me.

"Anna," she said, "when snowflakes tumble from the sky, they're more special than confetti on

New Year's Eve and more beautiful than a cloud of stardust."

My mom saw the good in everything.

The flakes invited me to join them on a walk to explore my new city of heart and grit. My initial inclination to decline ended when the building door slammed shut behind me. So, I headed out on a trifecta of firsts. First day in Chicago, first snow of the season, and the first time I met Marcella.

I worked my way up Michigan Avenue, awestruck by the splendor of the Wrigley Building, the Tribune Tower, and the whole magnificent skyline. After a while I took a detour over to State Street and discovered the small, eclectic shops, and smelled extraordinary aromas drifting from quaint restaurants.

My mood remained upbeat until I spotted my mom's reflection in the window of a small neighborhood store. I stopped to study the tilt of her head and dark, freewheeling brows, the same as mine. Her—*our*—small eyes peered at me and emphasized the fact I had outlived her by four years. An aneurysm dropped her to the kitchen floor one month to the day after her thirty-seventh birthday.

My shrink coined the word psycholepsy for these spells of mine, these abrupt visions that trigger mood changes accompanied by feelings of hopelessness, doom, and lethargy. To me, they're premonitions, ticks off the clock of life, reminding me I'm as vulnerable as my mom had been.

"A drink," I muttered, as I always do after an attack of psycholepsy, and ducked into the store for a bottle of gin. A little bell tinkled. Once inside, the door behind me hit the frame with a thud that felt like a commitment. I quickly dug into my pocket for a crumpled tissue to catch the flood of liquid that rushed from my nose due to the sudden change in temperature.

An old woman wearing a red beret sat behind a wooden checkout counter. A spindly display of cigarette cartons teetered behind her. She shifted her attention my way. My shoes shuffled over the wooden floor, reminding me of my childhood tap dance recitals.

Rather than heading straight for the booze, I lingered by the lettuce and thought back to my favorite performance. A star at age nine. The song I danced to was *Darktown Strutters' Ball*. My mom had made the costume, a pint-sized, red sequined tuxedo and top hat with a clip-on bowtie. She would have been twenty-nine then, only eight years left.

"You," the old woman barked. "If you just dropped in to look around, go to a museum."

"Chill," I said under my breath while picking up a head of romaine. Then I grabbed a bottle of Tanqueray and made my way to the checkout. I dumped them on the counter in front of her. "And a pack of Benson Hedges. Lights. Not menthol."

"Got an ID?"

"ID?" I launched a rare belly laugh. The first laugh since I stepped off the plane. It tickled me to pull the driver's license from my wallet and watch the old bat study it.

"My name's Anna Gerber, like the baby food," I said, like I always did, and rubbed my hands together to warm them. "How long do you have to live here to get used to the cold?"

The old lady eyed my flimsy jacket and leaned back, looking at me in the manner an artist studies a subject. "What kind of martini do you like?"

"Me?"

"Yes." She nodded toward the bottle.

Reluctant, I answered, "A Charles Dickens."

"No olive or twist," she said. "Ascetic choice."

"Ascetic?"

"Simple. Unembellished. Last night, I made Flying Dutchman's, with a drop of Curaçao." She pinched her fingers like squeezing a dropper.

I loosened up a little and took a good look at the woman. Her silver hair was drawn back under the beret, which sloped toward the left of her face—a face mapped of superhighways and main roads, with no trace of surface streets or shortcuts.

"We call those Cool Blue's where I'm from."

"California license," she said, handing it back to

me.

"They like 'em dirty in Sacramento?"

"The dirtier, the better," I said, almost tasting the olive juice in the gin. "What about you? You like them hot?"

"What do you mean, hot?"

"Jalapiñis. They're tequila with a jalapeño-stuffed olive."

"Had one once." She pinched her lips and shook her head. "Tequila has no business in a martini. You like 'em?"

I nodded with an apologetic shrug.

"My palate's more northern." Her brows shot up. "I'll tell you what." She pointed at me with a crooked finger stained with cash register ink. "If you find yourself thirsty around six, come back by. My place is upstairs. I've been drinking alone since Lulu died last July twenty-third. I'm sick and tired of drinking alone."

"Me too."

"Then you'll come?"

"See you then," I blurted, despite myself.

As I walked home, I quickly adopted the rushed pace of my fellow pedestrians, shoulders forward, face tucked down to shield it from the cold wind. It helped cut the chill but didn't cut the annoyance that ran through me for accepting the old lady's invitation.

I kept my distance from old folks, the same way

I steered clear of people with the flu, or chronic happiness. Old equals death. Death brings on sadness. Sadness turns into depression, and then I'm back to the shrink's office. But that lady had a strength I admired. Besides, it *was* my birthday. Not a day to drink alone.

I went back at six to have just one. The old woman rushed toward me when she heard the bell tinkle and the door slam. She greeted me with a strong and steady handshake.

"Jerry, meet Anna," she called to a hunched-over man stocking a low shelf.

He looked up and gave a nod.

"Jerry closes for me." She motioned for me to follow. "My place is upstairs."

The floor moaned as we inched through a messy storage room behind the shop, past stacked boxes that smelled of onions and garlic, and beets. We climbed the flight of stairs to a landing. A single bulb lit the area in front of a door painted citrus yellow.

The old lady slipped out of her work loafers and into a pair of fleece house shoes left next to the door. The entry led to the dining area. A brass candelabrum clutching eight candles sat on the center of a lace-covered table.

She fit her hand around the back of my arm and ushered me into her living room.

"Excuse the mess," she said and moved some

books from the couch to the floor. "I haven't had company since Lulu died."

I looked around. Several little-old-lady tea tables filled the space, each crammed with framed photos. She pointed to a blue wingback chair that faced the window. "If you sit there, dear, you'll be able to watch the people on the street. They never look up. Enjoy yourself while I mix your Charles Dickens. Tonight, I'll join you."

"Thank you, ma'am."

"Ma'am's no good. Call me Marcella. Last name's Kazarian. Rhymes with octogenarian."

My chest tightened at the sound of the word—octogenarian—double my age, and close to death for sure.

"I mix my martinis differently each time I have one," she said, as she pushed through a set of saloon-style shutter panels hinged to the kitchen doorframe. A *flap, smack* sound punctuated her exit.

I sat in the big, worn chair and looked out the window. Snow danced between me and the brick building across the way. Diners filled two cafes on the street level.

The chair smelled sour, so I got up to look at the pictures on one of the tea tables. I recognized some of the people from old movies I used to watch with my mom on the classic movie channel—Ray Bolger, Fred and Adele Astaire, William Powell and Myrna Loy. My mother cherished black-and-white movies.

I picked up one picture of Marion Davies and William Randolf Hearst lounging on a tiled patio, probably at his San Simeon mansion.

It didn't take long to realize that every one of those smiling people was dead, as dead as my mom. I set Davies and Hearst back and looked across the room, past the brocade couch, past the walnut coffee table, to the mantle over the fireplace. A man's portrait hung smack in the middle. Was it James Dean? *Dead, too.*

Marcella came back carrying a silver tray. Two frosted, classically-shaped martini glasses sat on it next to a silver shaker.

"Bombay Sapphire and Noilly Prat vermouth. Hope that's to your liking." She placed the tray on the coffee table and poured. She handed me a glass—an offering of hope to the forlorn.

"I want to make a toast to Lulu." She smiled, and the wrinkles around her eyes deepened. "We danced on Broadway together."

Marcella moved to one of the tables near the mantel and picked up a dusty picture. She turned toward me. "We danced in the chorus line of *George White's Scandals*. Lulu's the tall girl, third from the left. My best friend, for sixty-seven years."

She picked up a pack of matches and lit a cigarette. Wisps of smoke streamed out her mouth, then circled back. As if I'd stepped into a Felini film, the old lady French inhaled.

"And a toast to your birthday."

"How do you know it's my birthday?"

"From your driver's license," she said, cigarette in one hand, drink in the other. "If I may." She made a slight curtsy.

> *"'Tis better by far at the rainbows end*
> *to find not gold but the heart of a friend."*

I raised my glass and said, "To Lulu," and took a sip. The trademark taste of Noilly Prat rested nicely on my tongue. "You make a hell of a martini."

I wanted to say it's ridiculous to keep so many photographs of dead people around the house. And absurd to strike up new friendships when, at any time, a brain aneurysm could end it. Instead, I pretended to be interested in her pictures.

In one, a disheveled man stood between Lulu and Marcella.

"One of your boyfriends?"

"Oh, no, no. That's John Reed."

"John Reed, the Communist?"

"Yes."

"The one Warren Beatty played in *Reds*? The real one?"

She laughed. A laugh so pure and young sounding it seemed it hadn't aged along with the rest of her. She put out her cigarette, not even half-smoked, and set it on the ridge of a vintage crystal ashtray.

"Come sit on the couch, Anna."

We were close enough for me to see the threads of spider veins on her cheeks under translucent face powder. Three white hairs poked out from her chin.

"Now, where was I?"

"You said you're a Communist," I said, fascinated.

She flapped her hand as if to push aside my harebrained statement. "No, not really. We were young and did a lot of foolish things."

"But you knew John Reed."

"Met him a few times. A bit of a playboy."

"How'd you meet him?"

"Lulu and I ran with a cheeky crowd. We thought of ourselves as avant-garde New Yorkers, disgusted with the bourgeois society." She sipped her martini. "And, voilà, along came the Soviet Experiment."

"Soviet Experiment?"

"That's what they called it. Books about Russia became all the rage. We passed them around like romance novels and thought of ourselves as free thinkers."

"And you joined?"

She nodded. "The John Reed Club, at first. You didn't have to be a Communist, just a sympathizer."

"Wow."

"After a while, we filled out applications for the Party." She winked at me and tossed back the last of her drink. She looked at my empty glass. "Hold on, we need a refill."

While she went back into the kitchen, I thought about the movie *Reds*. Warren Beatty, Diane Keaton, the sweeping epic, the radical journalist, so charismatic and passionate that even I, just a kid when I saw it, wanted to follow him.

Marcella came back. I waited until she set the drinks down.

"Did you get in?"

"Get in where?"

"The Party. You and Lulu?"

"Of course we did." She picked up her glass and looked around the room for a specific picture, and raised her glass to it. "Salute to us. I miss you." She took a drink and continued. "We were young and good-looking, so we got assigned to the TTG."

"What's that?"

"The Theatrical Transient Group. Part of the la-de-da cultural division. Very elite."

"Elite Communists? Isn't that a contradiction?"

"I suppose it is." She chuckled. "But it only took two meetings for us to figure out Bolshevick fanatics are tedious and boring as hell. So, we ripped up our cards. Life went on."

The martinis exploded inside my head. Marcella steered the conversation back and forth through the years. During our third drink—or maybe the fourth?— she spoke with a tone of mystery about someone named Charles.

"Another drink?" she asked.

"No. I've already had too many." The cocktails and my day of moving hit me hard. "I only planned to have one. Just one. I have to say my goodbyes and find my way home."

I staggered heavy-footed down Michigan Avenue as the wind blew recklessly around my mood. Snow smothered the flowers and shrubbery in the concrete planters along the sidewalk.

"I predict you'll be dead by morning," I yelled to a cluster of frozen red coleus. "And you, too," I shouted at a car as it drove past. "And maybe me, too," I whispered.

Finally in bed, waiting for warmth to thaw my feet, I thought about the picture of James Dean, and, the ones of William Randolph Hearst and of John Reed. All dead. Charles somebody. Oldness. Mortality. Sleep.

Even though intrigued, I couldn't make myself go back to see Marcella. I thought it too risky, what with my "could-die-any-minute" phobia constantly hovering and the psycholepsy thing. But I did think of her often—who wouldn't?

Then, after two, or three months had passed, it happened again. My mother's reflection flashed in the window of a vacant shop. She looked angry, hands on hips.

"What?" I yelled at the window, like an aggressive street person high on something.

After I calmed down, I noticed a faded sign taped to the corner. It was sun-bleached and barely readable, and it said, "Marcella's Secret Closet - Last Chance Sale." My heart began to pound.

"What?" I yelled again looking back at the reflection. "You want me to go to *her*? This is insane. Why?"

"Because she'll help you," she said back. But she said it in my voice. I looked around. Two women crossed the street rather than pass by as I carried on with my discussion with the empty window.

That bizarre psycholepsy episode stayed with me. Actually, it haunted me until I finally decided my mom only wanted what was best for me.

From a table in the cafe across from Marcella's, I watched customers come and go from her store until precisely six o'clock when I got up and walked over.

"Hello, Anna," she said as if expecting me. She removed her apron, hung it on a hook next to the back door, and motioned for me to join her. "Jerry, we'll be upstairs."

As she opened the door to her apartment, she said, "When I worked on Broadway, the Bronx martini was all the rage. Gin with sweet and dry vermouth. Shall we try those tonight?"

I couldn't help but laugh. "The Bronx it is. Do you need any help?"

"I'm a pro." She went into the kitchen.

James Dean stared at me from the mantel. I turned my back to him and went to a table with the pictures of Marcella. Despite the years, no one could mistake her. How many years would it have been? Fifty? Sixty? So beautiful. Eyes shaped like crescents, dark hair parted down the middle. She looked to be a girl at ease in the center of attention.

In one photo, she donned a large peacock-feathered headpiece that fanned up and out. Other feathers cascaded down into a graceful skirt, slit up the front, her long legs exposed.

Marcella came from the kitchen and set the drinks on the coffee table. I picked up one and slugged down half of it.

"Anna, dear," she said, ignoring my bad manners. "I'm going to make a toast to Dorothy Parker. Actually, it's Dorothy Parker's toast." She grinned and recited in a theatrical tone.

> *I like to have a martini*
> *Two, at the very most*
> *After three, I'm under the table,*
> *After four, I'm under my host.*

Our glasses touched.

"Is she in any of these pictures?"

"Who?"

"Dorothy Parker."

"She never liked me." Marcella's top lip curled. "Gave me the snub."

"You knew some famous people," I said, as I looked around. "Tell me, is that who I think it is? The picture on your mantel?"

"If you think it's James Dean, then yes."

"Do you have a good story about him? Will you tell me?"

"Sometime I might, but not now."

"Ray Bolger?" I tried again.

"Why don't we talk about you tonight? Come sit on the couch."

As I looked at Marcella, I remembered some of the things my shrink had said: cultivate your relationships, make a difference to someone, and appreciate each era of life, blah, blah, blah. I had never taken the things he said seriously. Hell, I barely heard them.

Coming up with something to say took a minute. Then, I blurted out "I don't have friends like you had Lulu."

"Hard to believe."

"Well, this is my theory. Friends are like soap bubbles. You can't count on them to stay around too long."

"Poppycock, comparing friends to soap

bubbles." She looked at my empty glass but didn't offer a second. "Pure poppycock."

I should have excused myself and left, but instead, I closed my eyes and said, "When my mom died, I was forced to realize life is about loss."

"It's one aspect," she said softly. "Getting over those losses is another. It takes practice, but worth the effort. Everything takes practice."

I shrugged.

"I don't like your views of bubbles and friends," she scolded. "I think they're damn beautiful if you make the effort to look at them."

"I'm sure you're right," I said, but only to be polite.

"We can talk about friends another time," she said. "I'd like to announce that since we last saw each other, I invented a new martini called a Doctor Zhivago. Jewel of Russia vodka with a dollop of caviar in the glass. It's almost as delicious as Omar Sharif's smile."

"I invented a new one, too," I said, thankful for the change of subject. "I call it a Cold Cloud. I put a splash of Ouzo in a glass of Ketel One, and it turns milky."

"Brilliant. I have both in the kitchen. We'll try those next." Marcella leaned back and gazed around the room.

"Lulu and I started out in *The Scandals* the year Ray Bolger starred."

"Yes, you told me."

"Same year Ethel Merman starred in *Girl Crazy*. What a great dame she was. That show didn't last long, but the theater is still on Forty-Fifth Street. Someday, we'll go to New York and I'll show you the place."

I listened, taking pleasure in the effects of the drinks. Marcella didn't seem so old that evening. I found myself thinking how much fun it would have been to be friends with her and Lulu back then.

"Are you busy next Tuesday?" I asked.

That began our twice-a-week visits.

One evening, I stepped into Marcella's store and held up a jar of caviar I had bought especially for the evening, along with a bottle of Jewel.

"Doctor Zhivago's tonight," I said.

"Ossetra White caviar," she said, with a nod of approval.

"Fifty-nine dollars for this tiny little jar."

"What a treat." She rubbed her hands together. "Now, that's a good friend."

"My turn to make them," I said as we made our way into her apartment.

Liquor and condiments cluttered the kitchen counter. Vintage cocktail shakers and martini glasses crammed the open shelves to the left of the sink.

"Eat your heart out, Julie Christie," I said as I

emerged from the kitchen with the silver tray, Marcella style. I carried it to the living room and placed it on the coffee table. I plopped on the couch, nodded up at James and over at Lulu, relaxed into the cushions, and waited for another one of Marcella's stories.

"Why don't you tell me a little more about your mother," she said.

Reluctant at first, the words felt like rocks tumbling from my mouth. After a while, they slid out smoother. Talking about my mom had always sent me into a dark, sad temperament. Not that night.

The good stuff came out. The things she liked—passion fruit drizzled on ice cream, her old Karmann Ghia named Car Man. Spending hours going through catalogues and circling what she wanted with an orange crayon. How she practiced my tap routines with me, and taught me a dozen different versions of solitaire.

Discovering the high of talking about her freed me, but I didn't want to jinx the sensation.

"I've talked too much."

"She sounds like a beautiful bubble."

Yes, she was. Why don't we talk about one of your bubbles now."

"Which one? Lulu?"

"How about Charles?"

"Yes, *that's* a story," she said, patting my knee.

"Do you remember when I told you about the John Reed Club and all that communist chatter?"

"Of course."

"Well, as you might have suspected, there's more to the tale."

"Yes, I thought there had to be."

"It got a bit messy, all that McCarthyism business." She reached for a cigarette. "My glass is empty. This story calls for one more drink."

I took the glasses to the kitchen, threw together the vodka and caviar, filled a bowl with pretzels, and rushed back to my place on the couch.

"Where was I?"

"McCarthyism," I said, like a gossipmonger.

"Right, yes, you're so right. You've heard about the House Un-American Committee?"

I nodded.

"Those louts got their hands on Charles. Others, too. Subpoenaed them. No one was safe from their little, beady, probing eyes."

"Like *Guilty By Suspicion*? The De Niro movie?"

"A fiasco," she said, ignoring my question. "Stage lackeys. Bit actors. That's who they went after."

"Like De Niro," I said.

"They named the sham *The Broadway Hearings*. No one, absolutely no one apart from Charles cooperated."

"Your Charles?"

"Yes, indeed. My Charles. Didn't I tell you this?"

"No."

"Thirty years old when I met him. A scoundrel. A married one at that. I'm more than sure his wife made him squeal on everyone." She reached for a pretzel. "Charles gave me this building. Wait, I'm getting ahead of myself." She closed her eyes to concentrate. "Charles didn't mention Lulu or me. And, no one went to jail, but neither one of us worked in the theater again, thanks to Mrs. You-know-who. "

"He gave you this building? In Chicago?"

"He owned several buildings, as investments. He gave this one to me after the wife died in the late '60s. He felt he owed it to me for causing the end of my dance career." She paused, then said, "And, because I live here now, I suppose you could say Charles introduced us to each other."

The good news from corporate came at the end of August. They offered me a promotion, which meant relocating to Atlanta. Mixed emotions about the move consumed me. I thought of Marcella and our get-togethers. I'd changed because of her. I joined a gym, put a fish aquarium in my apartment, and no longer felt weighed down with doom. I imagined a future and started buying lottery tickets, using the numbers below the sayings on fortune cookies.

How would she take the news? How could I relocate without her?

On our last evening together, Marcella and I strolled arm-in-arm toward the Ambassador Hotel to have dinner in the Pump Room. Despite the summer heat, she wore a chinchilla boa draped around the neck of her dress. Four limp paws dangled from one shoulder.

Old pictures of movie stars and Chicago notables lined the corridor into the restaurant.

"Look, Anna," Marcella pointed. "There's Norma Talmadge. My mother took me to see her in *The Only Woman*. She was the first one to press her footprints in the cement out front of Grauman's Chinese."

Once served, Marcella pushed the sweet peas and glazed carrots around the plate with her fork, not touching the veal fillet.

"I've been thinking," she finally said, "or rethinking your soap bubble theory. You might be right after all." Her eyes traveled past me toward the front of the room, and her shoulders slumped.

"Poppycock," I said battling a dozen impulses to tell her I'd stay. "What do you say we finish the evening with a martini at the piano bar?"

We both ordered a Charles Dickens.

"A toast to my friend," I said and lifted my

glass.

> *I like to have a cocktail,*
> *Four, at the very least*
> *With my friend Marcella,*
> *Who's made my life a feast.*

I promised to return for her birthday.

We spoke on the phone almost every Saturday morning. She gave me a new martini recipe each week: a Bully Pulpit, a Silent Night, a Que Sera. Even one for Thanksgiving called the Gobble Gobble, with three pomegranate seeds. "I'm experimenting with a purple martini," she said. "The color of Liz Taylor's eyes. Needs more work. Maybe when I feel better."

One Saturday, she didn't answer the phone. I tried again on Sunday and began to worry. Relief came when I got home from work on Tuesday to find a package from Marcella at the front door. Inside, a beige envelope rested on Styrofoam packing squiggles. She had written "My Gerber Baby" across the front of it. I pulled on the flap and ripped it open. Marcella's embossed initials rose from the note card.

Anna dear,

I'm sick and tired of drinking alone. I thought about coming to Atlanta to visit you, and then thought it better to go see Lulu and Charles. I'm taking my favorite

martini shaker, my old dancing shoes, and my beret.
I'll never forget our friendship. You helped me.

When you're an old woman, you will probably look back on your life as a first draft. As unrefined and incomplete as it might seem, please remember that it reads like a classic novel with a martini in your hand.

P.S. When one phase of your life ends, please move on to the next. And may it be everything you want it to be.

With Love,
Marcella

I dropped the card and reached for the phone. The buttons blurred through my tearing eyes, and it took several tries to get through.

"You have reached a number that is no longer in service."

I didn't touch the box until the following evening at our time, six o'clock. Inside, a silver martini shaker, a silver strainer, and two martini glasses. I reached further down through the squiggles and discovered a worn notebook bulging with recipes and yellowed scraps of paper. Handwritten on each page, she'd put the date, the name of her concoction, and her recipe with special notations for variations. The first page was for The Bronx, dated February 8, 1935.

I mixed an impromptu martini to be forever known as The Marcella. Grey Goose vodka with a splash of Chambord dancing on the surface. A classy and elegant drink.

"To you, Marcella." I raised my glass. "May your reunion with Lulu, Charles, and all the dancers be everything you want it to be. If you bump into my mom, be sure to tell her you're my friend."

Face Down In The Grady River

The Waitress

The July heat shot through the Grinnin' Possum cafe and stuck to every pore on Tilly Washington's body. She grabbed a tissue from the sleeve of her waitress uniform to wipe the humidity from the creases of her dark neck. She patted the hairline of her nappy curls, then rubbed the water spots off the prongs of a fork before tucking the tissue back into her sleeve.

All the morning regulars had gone except Mrs. Quincy, who sat at the lunch counter drinking an

Orange Nehi from a chipped glass. Tilly didn't bother to switch it out, figuring the woman couldn't see the chip because her bifocals were forever perched on her rust-colored updo like an unusual tiara.

On Thursdays, Mrs. Quincy's house girl saw to the heavy cleaning, and rather than remain home during the ordeal, she stayed at the cafe clear through the lunch rush.

"Damnedest thing happened," she said as she watched Tilly wipe a clot of gravy off the counter. "Damnedest thing you ever heard."

"What's that, Mrs. Quincy?"

"They found Stiles Pitts face down in the Grady River. Face down, Tilly, face down."

"What are you talkin' about?" Tilly looked into Mrs. Quincy's green eyes rimmed with smudged mascara.

"Drowned, Tilly, drowned in waist-high water while fishing with his yellow mutt Digger right by his side."

The news rattled the boredom right out of Tilly. Stiles Pitts was her biggest tipper.

"Pitts?"

Mrs. Quincy nodded.

"Not Pitts," Tilly said, concerned. "He's my biggest tipper. You sure?"

"But the real kicker is." Mrs. Quincy took a long sip of her Nehi and placed it back on the counter before continuing. "Folks say they found a dead peacock near his body."

This was not good news. It stirred Tilly's insides and promised to lighten her pockets something awful. She wanted to know a lot more about Stiles Pitts drowning all by himself but wasn't about to fuel Mrs. Quincy's tendency to fiddle with rumors. The dead peacock portion of the story was more than likely a spoonful of the lady's own personal, fictitious icing on the story.

Tilly figured after her shift, she'd head to The Razor's Edge, next to the sheriff's station, where the deputies got sheared and shaved, and their official tongues wagged freely about such matters.

It was common knowledge that old man Pitts went to the Grady River every day. In his tackle box he packed a tube of Pringles and a twelve-ounce tin of Spam, along with a bottle of fig brandy. He possessed a natural gift for spotting the biggest fish in the river and plucked them out with a honey-colored bamboo rod with a worn cork grip.

While Tilly wondered how Pitts could have drown in that shallow river, a lopsided man in plaid trousers came through the squeaky door. As he moved past the Formica tables, a tap on the sole of his shoe scraped the floor, followed by the thud of his cane. *Scrape, then thud, scrape, then thud.*

He wobbled his way to the lunch counter. Two

stools separated the man and Mrs. Quincy. She twisted to brush an imaginary something off her shoulder while eyeing him. Then she looked at Tilly.

"Who in hell? You ever seen him before? I'm askin, who in hell, Tilly?" She didn't say it through a bullhorn, but she might as well have.

Tilly shrugged and shook her head, but she did know exactly who he was—Wesley Haze. He'd been around for years but stayed mostly to himself. She'd seen him from a distance a few times, hobbling around by the bridge near her house, but she'd never seen him up close before.

Tilly offered a menu to the broken man, then set it on the counter when he didn't reach to accept it. A nose full of catfish and hush puppies frying in lard replaced the morning smell of sweet potato pie.

"The Grinnin' Possum's happy you're here," she said, the same as she said to everyone.

Wesley Haze nodded and steadily drummed his fingernails on the table. Tilly set a glass of water in front of him. Her large hand brushed against his tapping fingers. His eyes opened as big as quarters. She smiled and passed him a nod, her well-practiced tip nod.

She thought she saw the lines around his mouth relax in the one second before he swung the glass to his lips, licked the rim, and slurped the water. His free hand reached into his pants pocket and jiggled the change inside. She heard it as the sweet sound of a gratuity.

"Noisy SOB," Mrs. Quincy barked. "You ever hear that much noise comin' off a person? Sounds like a one-man band without the washboard, if you ask me."

Tilly had limited experience in guessing the age of white folks. He could have been thirty-five, or he could have been fifty. Rows of scalp ran through the furrows of his freshly combed hair. What looked to be a collapsed jawbone caused his mouth to pull to the left. Tilly noticed his tar-black pupils glide past her, and stare off. It struck her, he could be blind, what with the cane and all.

She leaned over the counter, real close to his face, to get a better look. "How about I start you off with our lunch special? A bowl of green turtle soup."

"Yes, please." Haze looked up and nodded five or six times like his head was attached to a spring. He could see just fine.

When Tilly set the soup on the counter, he hunched over the bowl as if it were a vaporizer and inhaled deeply. He closed his eyes. His face began to flush and turned as slick as a carefully polished nectarine.

"What in hell?" Mrs. Quincy said and shook her head, watching the man real careful. "What in hell's he doin'?" She turned to see if anyone else was in the cafe witnessed the same thing. "He looks like a dog with his head in the bowl. Like a dog."

The woman rarely held back when the opportunity arose for bad manners. Tilly figured Mrs. Quincy's mean-spirited remarks stemmed from a need to ensure her own importance.

After Mrs. Quincy said what she said, the man pulled himself back upright in the chair, crushed a packet of saltines, and sprinkled them into the soup. He waited until the cracker nuggets soaked up the juice and went limp, then stabbed at them with the spoon.

The business about Stiles Pitts still used up most of Tilly's concentration, but she took a moment to stand back and notice the ticks, taps, smacks, and wheezes bursting from Wesley Haze. Primal sounds, she thought, as uncontrolled as gospel, or jazz coming from a bass guitar. She heard his music, and thought she knew it as well as she knew her own symphony of belittlement. Tilly held great affection for the undervalued.

The jingling of change in Wesley Haze's pocket brought her thoughts back to the treasure that'd soon be hers.

The Customer

Haze sat straight, tightened his jaw, and prepared for another unfavorable remark from the lady to his left.

"Don't pay no mind to Mrs. Quincy over there. How ya'll doin today?" the waitress asked. She had a small voice for such a large woman. The words slid out lean, and shadowy, and confidential-like.

"Fine." The word blew out like a belch. He softened his voice and tried again. "Just fine."

He glanced up. The woman's puffy eyes reminded him of charred walnuts, and the freckles splattered across her flat nose resembled the Big Dipper. Haze wanted to say, "I like your nose," but he didn't.

He looked back into his soup bowl to calm his nerves and studied the lifeless cracker parts. Haze heard Bo Diddly singing "Hand-Jive" as loud and clear as if the record whirled inside his bowl. He tapped out the beat with his left hand. *He's got a cool little chick named Rockin' Millie…Doin that crazy hand jive.*

For all the commotion he made, it rarely came from words. That was partly due to a busted jaw from a beating he took as a kid and partly because he didn't get much practice. People rarely glanced his way, let alone spoke to him. But the waitress had. Her voice trespassed his edgy shield with a tone of intimacy he'd rarely experienced before.

"Hotter than hellfire today, isn't it?" she said, as she fanned herself with a menu. "My name's Tilly. If you want anything else, just ask."

He followed the movement of the menu-fan and

studied her hand. He recalled the touch of it, the surprise of it. He drifted... *got a cool little chick named Rockin' Tilly.*

For most of his life, he'd struggled with panic, and when it happened, Haze slipped into a privacy that eclipsed time and place. He leaned into the hot breath of the soup, and his mind wandered back to the previous day, when he'd first spotted the peacock.

As he walked along the edge of the Grady River, watching the water flap on the banks, he heard squawks in the distance. He soon came upon a big, blue cock on the branch of an oak tree draped with moss. Like a hungry buzzard, its focus was set on the fisherman and the yellow mutt below.

Haze wanted to tell the waitress named Tilly about the episode—no one else, just her. But he couldn't gather the courage to lift his head up from the soup bowl. The next best thing was to *imagine* himself telling her.

It wouldn't be at the cafe. More likely they'd be walking through the Absolution Music Depot and Liquidators, where he worked as the night watchman. He'd recount, just between the two of them, all that happened on the Grady River.

The Absolution Music Depot housed relic jukeboxes. Jukes silent as frozen clocks since their owners traded them in for newer models. Haze would walk the waitress named Tilly through the warehouse and show her his favorite, a 1942 antique Wurlitzer. He would press the chunky buttons and show her how the lights flexed to the music. *Doin that crazy hand jive.*

He and the girl with the walnut eyes would dance in the cavernous building. It would be a dance of trust that smelled of jasmine and crepe myrtle. Then he would speak to her.

"What do you do when not serving up smiles and kind words at the cafe?"

"I collect trinkets," she would answer.

"Trinkets?"

"Yes. I pick 'em out of dumpsters or gutters and stick 'em in my backpack."

"What kind of trinkets?"

"Whatever I can get my hands on. I don't mind reaching into my sack of tip change when I have to. I like broken things," he would hear her say in that soft voice.

"Where do you live?"

"On the other side of town, over the narrow bridge where the river bends, and the pavement turns to dirt."

It wouldn't seem peculiar at all that the girl who smelled of Jasmine and danced light as the wind lived by the very spot where he came across the old fisherman.

Being prone to those kinds of daydreams was

another reason Haze kept quiet. He struggled to sort true-to-life occurrences from his made-up stories. He could never be sure which was which.

He first learned about made-up stories from his mama. She'd nestle her lips close to his ear and stroke his hair while reciting tales to him about beauty and love like the one about the snake-skinned rabbit who didn't fit in until she met the family of piglets who thought she was lovely, and the one about the Unicorn who only allowed people with true hearts to see her.

His mama said that when you tell made-up stories your heart forgets about aching and invites you to join in on holidays that no one else knows about. She kept pebbles in the tin box hid under her bottom dresser drawer, one for every story they shared.

Thin as a tree swallow, she did her best to keep close watch over him. Haze always saw the hope she held for him in her moist blue eyes. She left one night with the tin box, the year Haze turned seven. The same year he got polio, and his daddy's rage turned toward him. That's when he began to make-believe his daddy was dead and imagine his way to safety.

Haze would tell the waitress how he came upon the fisherman while picking up the kind of pebbles his mama liked. The sun burned hot, and the air was thick with moisture. The kind of weather that conjures up scorn.

The old man was stupid full of liquor. He raised his arm toward the tree, pointed at the peacock, and cussed at it in the same hateful manner Haze's daddy used to do. The bird stretched its long neck forward and gave out that most god-awful sound only peacocks make. The man's yellow mutt barked like a machine gun and scratched at the tree trunk. The cock's tail heaved skyward, flashing green and gold.

Haze would hear the waitress named Tilly say, in a voice as sweet as his mama's, "Heavens! Them peacocks can get crazy. Then what happened?"

He would show her a pebble from his pocket, and they would continue to dance in their private shelter of acceptance, while he'd tell her how he crouched behind a stump thick with new sprouts, with his boots settled an inch into the mud so not to be seen.

He'd tell her the old fisherman took the tube of chips out of his tackle box, burrowed his hand inside the canister, and pulled two out. He turned one upside down to form a Pringles duckbill and stuck them in his mouth. His shoulders jumped, and his arms flapped, and he began to quack. The dog got fiercely excited.

The potato chips jutting from the fisherman's mouth set the bird off like his dignity had been called to task. His squawks turned so thunderous Haze had to cover his ears. The fisherman spit the chips into the water, picked up his fishing pole, cocked it like a baseball bat, and took a wild swing toward the bird. He walked knee-high into the river for a better angle and took another swing.

The contempt in the old man's eyes took Haze's mind back to the times his daddy used to beat his mama. But unlike the bird, she never had the nerve to screech or charge. She thought better than to challenge the unsound.

Right then, on the side of the Grady River, Haze resolved to make things right. His mama had deserved better, and so had he.

His pockets were heavy with pebbles—one for every bruise caused by the turn of a switch, and one for every drunken rage. He began to throw them at the fisherman, or was it his daddy? None hit their mark. The old man's attention was on the bird and nothing else. Haze stepped out from behind the stump and moved closer.

He spotted a cluster of fist-sized stones alongside a chinaberry tree. He picked one up and threw it hard as he could. As fast as that, the fisherman dropped his pole, clutched his shoulder, and stumbled back toward the river bank, confused by what happened. He lost his balance, landed on the empty brandy bottle next to his tackle box, and let out a moan. He got himself up on his knees and saw Haze. Their eyes caught. Realizing where the rock had come from, he pointed at Haze with both hands, his thumbs cocked. His drunken eyes flashed with spite.

Haze picked up another rock and threw it to make things right. He scored a bull's eye to the forehead just as the bird charged the man. The yellow mutt got to the bird first and clamped his jaw around its neck. The two of them zigzagged through the water, then slammed into the man, or was he already down? The mutt had the upper hand over the cock, and the shallow water of the Grady River churned with commotion.

Haze remained stone still until the mutt finished with the bird. Then he limped toward home, his back to the riverbank smothered with iridescent blue-green feathers. Stiles Pitts remained face down, with an empty tin of Spam floating next to his body.

"Mister, you okay? Is everything okay, mister?"

He realized he was at the lunch counter, bent over a bowl of turtle soup, and didn't know how long he'd been there.

Wesley Haze looked up. The waitress named Tilly, the one he may have danced with and might have told his story to, said, "You okay?" She said it sweet as syrup but looked concerned.

He couldn't be sure if he'd drifted into one of

his episodes or if the incident at the Grady River had been a genuine recollection. He supposed that only the yellow mutt knew for sure.

"Like a dog," Mrs. Quincy said. "A dog with his head in a bowl, you ever seen such a thing, Tilly?"

The Waitress

Scrape, then thud, scrape, then thud.

Wesley Haze headed for the front door. He hadn't said a word since Tilly brought him the soup. Her mood dropped when she realized the sweet jingle of tip change on the counter never reached her ear. But, when she cleared off his mess, she found a twenty-dollar bill next to the soup bowl.

A grin, matched only by the possum on the sign out front, hit her face. She figured her share to be close to seventeen dollars, far more than anything Pitts ever left. She stuck the money in her apron pocket and hoped to goodness that the broken man would stop by again.

Then her mind went back to wondering how in the world Stiles Pitts could have drowned face down in the Grady River while fishing with his yellow mutt, Digger.

Fasten Your Seat Belt

Doctor Mulrooney never looks straight at me. He sits behind his big desk, studies his fingernails, and begins to pick at them just before talking to me.

"You're no longer a little girl. You're twenty-four." He says this like I don't already know.

He thinks I worry too much. He says, "It's time you learn to recognize the difference between perceived danger and real danger," which, of course, makes me worry about what he means. I wish he'd look at me, but instead he just picks and talks, and talks. When I think he's almost done, more words come out. "We must look at the cultural processes that influence your perception of what constitutes danger . . ."

Those words are all I can think about, with the plane engine sounding too loud—like it's straining. Because I'm flying alone in seat 18B, it's hard to know if I'm experiencing actual danger, or not.

I'll just look at the clouds. From up here, they remind me of cotton ballss, like the ones stored inside the jars that sit on the cart, right next to the sterilization liquid.

When I close my eyes, I still see the puffy billows on the inside of my lids, only each one's a different color. I can smell them too. No, that smell is from the airplane, and it makes me nervous—the same kind of nervous like when I overheard those two women in the airport restroom talking about plane crashes.

My day started off all wrong because of them. They both stood in front of the sinks, looking at each other in the mirror. The tall one wiped water spots off the counter. Her face looked like a paint-by-numbers portrait filled in by someone who wasn't very good at staying inside the lines. I don't admire that look.

While she put on her lipstick, she told her friend, the gray lady that she'd read a newspaper article about pilot incompetence. Her friend nodded her head in agreement and said she only books aisle seats because, if the plane blows up, she'll have someone to hold on to, but in a window seat, she'll end up sucked straight out of the plane, all alone.

I wanted to say, "If you can't say something nice about flying, don't say anything at all," but I just watched them until they were finished. The gray lady didn't even wash her hands before she left.

If Doctor Mulrooney had been there, he would have told me to stop my excess worrying and recognize that those ladies were demonstrating symptoms of catastrophic expectations. He'd say, like he always does, I'm old enough to understand that nothing they said was grounded in reality. Nevertheless, it's all their fault my day is going so bad. I thank God they're not on this flight.

Oh, grape nuts for breakfast, there's a vibration under my shoes. It's coming from what I imagine to be the cargo hold, even though I don't know where the cargo hold is. The vibration feels like a tremor trying to work itself into a very large seizure. Clutching my hands to the armrests doesn't help.

I'll just close my eyes and think about what kind of tattoo I would get, if I were ever to get one. That should keep my mind off the stuff that bothers me, like seizures, turbulence, and unexpected, sudden drops in altitude.

I used to think about my name. About what I would change it to if I were ever to change it. My parents are hard-working, well-meaning people, but I can't even fathom what they were thinking when they named me. Zoey Patroni, geeze, what a name. It's their fault the other kids teased me.

It started in kindergarten. I still remember that scrawny little boy, Ian, pestering me. I remember his Cheeto-stained hands that matched his freckles and hair. I remember him pointing one orange finger at me and then shaking it. And all the while, he'd cup his crotch with his other hand as he jumped around singing the Oscar Mayer tune with the words, "My patroni has a first name – it's Z-O-E-E-Y."

He jumped and twirled around all the kids in line for snacks and got them to sing along. And Ian used to beat me to the supply room during craft class. He'd take the happy colors, leaving only black for me.

I hope Ian grew up with chronic, hideous Cheeto breath. I know it's his fault the other kids laughed at me and stayed away from me.

Doctor Mulrooney would probably say it's time to move beyond my grudge, but Doctor Mulrooney's an idiot. He's the kind of idiot who's intellectual, but not intelligent. He went to fancy schools and wears a white coat all day, but that doesn't mean he has the intelligence to cut the hairs hanging out of his nose.

Aside from the hairs, his nose isn't that bad. *My* nose is horrible. It doesn't match anything on my face. My eyes are small, and my lips are thin, but boy, oh boy, my nose goes on forever. One thing's for sure—I have enough intelligence to cut my nose hairs if I had any, which I don't.

Oh, grapenuts, there I go again. I've fallen off the subject. Maybe I'll have my tattoo say, "Zoey Patroni is full of bologna." It's most likely what crosses everyone's mind when they hear my name.

I'll have the words tattooed on my upper arm, under a gorgeous red and turquoise wiener mobile with a banner streaming around it. I'll go sleeveless for the whole world to see I'm not afraid of being called that.

Tattoos are more than just pigment on the flesh. Before I started going to The Immaculate Heart Tattoo Parlor, I didn't think of tattoos as art. Now, I've come to realize they bring color and light to the soul.

The first time I walked in the place, I was nervous as could be. A big fluffy cat had plopped down close to the doorway, so I stepped over it. I couldn't help but wonder what kind of tattoos were under that ball of gold and white fuzz. That cat couldn't care less what I thought, and it looked up at me with big yellow who-gives-a-damn-eyes.

The artist, that's what they call themselves,

tattoo artists, was cleaning the studio. They're called studios, not parlors. Her lipstick looked black. I found myself hoping it was lipstick instead of a lip tattoo. Her dark, straight hair swayed as she sprayed something blue, like disinfectant, on the display counter. She spread it around with a paper towel in slow circles. She acted like I was invisible, so I stood still as though I was. But, boy, was I nervous.

I smelled flea powder and Lysol, which reminded me of sterilization liquid. After some thought, that made sense because tattoo studios have a lot of needles.

The walls were filled with so many things that I got dizzy and sat on a sofa covered with black and white cowhide. I admired the softness of that sofa, and bounced on it a little.

I admired everything in that studio except the artist's lips. She had a tattoo of the Mad Hatter on her left arm. Underneath it were the words, "Mad as a Hatter." It tickled my fancy, and I laughed out loud. The cat looked up, but the artist kept right on cleaning.

I was too nervous to ask where the rabbit and Alice were, but I didn't have to ask about the little shamrocks on her right hand. The whole world knows that shamrocks bring good luck. She looked like she might need some good luck, just like me.

After a while, she said a couple of things to me,

but she talked mostly to the cat. Her voice was as smooth as the white streams of cigarette smoke coming out of her mouth. When her lips moved, the sound seemed to come from somewhere else. She said her name was Lubella, and she called the cat Trixie Treasure.

The walls of The Immaculate Heart were colorful as can be, covered with flash sheets. That's what they call the square papers that show the tattoo designs. There are no special rules about what you pick from the flash, and if you don't see anything that suits your fancy, you can bring in your own design.

Some of the flash looked real nice at the start. But when I studied them closely, instead of a happy little wizard or gnome, I saw things I hadn't noticed at first: skeleton heads, winged bats, fire and octopus tentacles, and on and on. As soon as that happened, I remembered back to when Doctor Mulrooney told me I should try to face my fears. Then, I stepped back and squinted, and the scary stuff returned to harmless wizards or gnomes.

A few of the designs on the walls were from famous ink slingers. That's what they call the good ones. Just make sure you don't go to a scratcher.

Lubella told me she knew some of the famous ones, like Hanky Panky and Shotsie Gorman, Mr. Cartoon, and there's even someone called Spider Webb. I doubt they're their real names.

If you ask me, Lubella's the famous one. Clowns are her specialty. The wall behind the cow loveseat is covered floor to ceiling with flash of clowns and circus performers. Lubella's very own designs. My favorite has butterfly wings and a big ball-and-chain holding him down. Lubella calls him Gabriel. She said his design has thirty-three different hues, and the piece is like a portrait of a tortured soul.

I like Gabriel because that's the way I feel sometimes. I want to spread my wings and travel around, but I get stuck and sad. Lubella says tattoos are called travel marks. They show you've been around and had some life experience like I want to.

Oh, grapenuts for lunch. The "fasten your seat belt" sign just lit up. I keep my belt fastened all the time anyway. It feels safer to be strapped in. I don't like this turbulence, and I wish the pilot would stop talking on the microphone and get back to flying the plane. He sounds like Doctor Mulrooney, with a voice that's supposed to make you feel better, but doesn't.

My mind needs to get back to my tattoo. Lubella doesn't think I'll ever get a tat because I'm too nervous. I know somewhere in my soul I'm a colorful, free spirit trying to spread my wings, like Gabriel.

Doctor Mulrooney says that circumstances are never out of my control if I take control. Right now, I'm taking my time to decide which tattoo will best represent my personal expression. Besides, thinking about my tattoo keeps my mind off the stuff that bothers me, like cotton swabs and sterilization liquid before injections.

Maybe my tat will be a boa constrictor. A big one. I'll have it done in electric tones like hot pink and ultraviolet. It will wrap around my body, slither up from my left ankle, around my left thigh, across my left buttock over to the right side of my waist and around my torso, then work its way between my breasts and rest its forked tongue just short of that soft, sensitive spot on my neck that makes me absolutely out of my mind when someone, who shall remain nameless, kisses me there. I mean hot-to-trot out of my mind. Just thinking about it makes my mouth water and does funny things to my nipples, and—oh my goodness, it seems that I've taken an off-ramp here and need to get myself back on the freeway.

Once, I had a dream about getting a tattoo. In the dream, I asked Dr. Mulrooney what kind he'd get if he were to get one. He scolded me and went on a tirade about the scriptures—Leviticus 19:28. Not just the name and number, but the entire scripture. *You shall not make any cuttings in your flesh . . .or tattoo any marks upon you.* In the dream he sounded like Sister Mary Ignatius.

In school, Sister Mary Ignatius used to quote trick scriptures to try to make me behave. If that didn't work, she'd give me assignments I couldn't understand, and then she'd call me stupid in front of the other kids. When you think about, it's probably Sister's fault that the other kids laughed at me, and stayed away from me.

Ian was her favorite student in the class because they were both Irish. Doctor Mulrooney's Irish, too. The Irish hate Italians. It's a known fact.

Oh, nuts, nuts, grapenuts, I hear the lunch cart coming through. I don't like that sound. It makes me nervous. I am feeling a lot of turbulence inside my body. I am strapped in, but the noise of that cart is one of my biggest fears.

******

Sandra's here with the lunch cart and the little cup of medication marked 18B, my bed number. She knows I spent the whole morning by myself, and she'll ask if I've had a nice day. I'll tell her about my flight and the ladies in the restroom, and she'll realize why I'm feeling so nervous.

Sandra's just like Lubella. They could be sisters —twins. Her hair sways in circles when she cleans my tray, and I like to watch her mouth move when she talks. She says nice things to me, except when she gives me that look and tells me I must try to keep my mind on circumstances that are real and not just made up inside my head.

If I were a cat like Trixie Treasure, I'd want to live with her. Sandra and Lubella both make their living poking needles into flesh and making people feel better about themselves.

Sandra says she likes men who wear uniforms. Me too. I like the Sparkletts man. I'd like him to kiss me on that spot on my neck.

Every afternoon, I sit by the window to watch him pull up in front of the ward to deliver the water. His truck has rippled silver metal on the sides that sparkles when the sun hits just right. It looks like metallic rain.

Anyway, Sandra says other things, too. She doesn't like those two cleaning ladies, the gray one and the one with the painted face. She says there's no reason for them to say some of the things they say, especially around the patients.

Her hair will sway when she gives me that look to let me know everything will get better. I'm strapped in, and that's how I like it, but I wonder about Sandra. I think she's Irish.

Fate Carries Its Own Clock

"There's nothin' wrong with takin' a ride in a hearse so long as you're sittin' up front."

Uncle Mooks said that every time one of those funeral parades drove by, being that our house was dead center between the Faith Deliverance Holy Church and the graveyard.

We'd sit on the front porch every Sunday afternoon, him on the couch stuffed with springs and tree moss, and me on the swing. We watched as the cars with their headlights set on high beams drove past, slow and steady as a family of box turtles.

"Jason Lee," he'd say. "The clock of life's always tickin' towards the Last Breath Funeral Parlor, so whatever you do, make sure you stay one step ahead of that second hand. You know what I'm sayin', son?" I'd look into his vacant blue eyes and bob my head like I did know.

Melvin Orville Oswald Kastor, Mooks for short, had been to Vietnam and back. Over there, that second hand tapped him on the shoulder, but he fought like hell to get away. To prove it, he had a scar on his left temple with a dent the size of a quail egg and a disposition that seemed like a kid and a wise man, all in one. Sometimes after too many Falstaff's, he'd point to his scar and say, "Jason Lee, don't never get on the wrong side of a gook's bayonet. And, don't never go fight a war drummed up by a room full of politicians who don't have the balls to call it a war. Conflicts are for talkin' out. You hear me son? Vietnam conflict, my ass."

Mama would come out to check on us if Uncle Mooks got too rambunctious about Vietnam or some of the other things that got him riled. She'd stroke his bushy hair and knead his shoulder muscles, then sing an old song they used to know when they were kids. It was hard to see how those two were brother and sister, let alone twins unless you caught them smiling at the same time. Both their mouths turned downward, and their chins filled with tiny dimples.

Her life sure had changed because of that Vietnam conflict. My daddy never came back, and she got Uncle Mooks full-time. You could say she had to raise the both of us.

It must have been more than terrible for her. On a Wednesday, two uniformed officers knocked on our door with the news about my daddy, and the very next day came the phone call that Uncle Mooks was coming home but needed special care.

I never knew Uncle Mooks before he suffered his head wound, but there was no doubt he still knew things from back then, like how to recognize the calls of the first purple martins to arrive in spring. He showed me how the birds fashioned their nests and laid one pure white egg each sunrise for five days. He showed me how to scoop up the spiders and mosquito hawks and carry them outside before Mama got to them with a fly swatter. And even though he hadn't left our property since the day he came back from Vietnam, he told me where to dig for the best fishing worms.

We played stare-down, no blinking and no flinching. The trick was, don't look at your opponent's eyes, focus on the eyebrows. He taught me that a stare-down is part of the basic training of life and not to rush it because time's either for you or against you. He'd say, "Time makes the decision, not you." He had a real thing about time and always carried his prized possession with him, a gold pocket watch.

Family traditions are one thing, but by the time I turned thirteen, that front porch began to feel like a prison. I'd decided there had to be more to do in life than spend Sundays watching funeral parades and cutting up empty Falstaff cans with tin snips to form them into wind spinners. Uncle Mooks hung his spinners in the cypress trees that grew throughout our property.

That's when I started spending more time with Samson. The kids at school had finally grown tired of bullying us for being best friends.

One day, we were headed home after school. Summer vacation was close enough you could smell it in the dogwoods. We were in no particular hurry when we heard a ruckus from behind and knew it was his little brother Elijah pedaling up on his bike, sure as we knew it was the king of spades strumming the front wheel and the king of clubs on the back. Then, a pillow of dust swelled as Elijah shot right past, acting like he didn't even see us in the middle of the road. Not a nod or a hello. Nothing.

"Where's he goin' so almighty fast?" I asked.

He looked straight ahead, like he was studying

Elijah's dust, and shrugged his shoulders.

"What's that mean?"

"Means what it means."

"Mean you don't know?"

"No."

"What's it mean, then?"

"Means don't ask no questions. It's none of your damn business."

I stopped in the road and spoke right in Samson's face. "The clock of life speeds up and cheats you out of precious time when you try to withhold information."

He looked at me. "The clock of life, Jason Lee? You gone crazy on me? You're soundin' like that uncle of yours."

"Okay," I said, realizing he was right. "I'm gonna ask you straight out again. Where's Elijah headed in such an almighty hurry?"

The both of us stood there, fixed in a full-blown stare-down. Samson's bulging brown eyes peered from his black face down the four inches it took to meet my firm, blue-eyed glare. I knew Samson couldn't win. My eyes were trained from years of practice with Uncle Mooks. That was my first try away from the front porch.

It took some time, but Samson finally glanced away. I said, "I think what's goin' on here is we're havin' a conflict. And conflicts are for talkin' out."

It wasn't long before he said, "He's headed to

Grover Peek's pond."

The words hit me hard.

Mama had told me to stay clear of the likes of Grover Peek. I'd never actually set eyes on the man, but for sure I'd never heard a good word about him either.

It was common knowledge that he and my daddy never saw eye to eye. Peek was part of the old-school Klan types, and it seems my daddy stirred up a hornet's nest when he went off to join a freedom march.

I didn't know too much about him, but Mama once told me, "Your daddy was always so almighty sure of what was right and wrong. And he was strong-willed enough to stand up to all them closed-minded bastards like Grover Peek."

And then, one day, Uncle Mooks handed me an old, limp piece of newspaper. "This is about him."

I kept that article, along with my daddy's congressional army medal, in a box under my bed. I memorized the words by heart, about him being 'a white man strong willed enough to walk with the blacks and not drag his feet toward the certain road to integration.' Since I never really knew him, sometimes it felt like the article was about a stranger.

"Grover Peek's place?" I practically yelled. "Is he crazy? What if the old man catches him?"

Samson kicked the dirt. "He ain't gonna get caught."

"He's your brother? I said in frustration. "And Grover Peek's the meanest bastard in these parts. What kind of stupid is that?"

"I couldn't do nothin'. I told him he was on his own. But I didn't think he'd really go there."

"So, tell me, what possessed him to do that?"

"Wants to swim but don't know how."

"Swim? Swimmin's easy."

"Not if you don't know how."

"You know how?"

"Nope."

"How'd you get to be thirteen without knowin' that?"

I walked over and grabbed him by the shoulders, all the while thinking about the skull-and-crossbones no-trespassing signs posted around Grover Peeks land. There were plenty of those signs.

"There's lots of ponds around. Why on earth go to this one? What's he thinkin'?" I said.

"I don't think he's thinkin'."

"I can teach the both of you to swim. There's plenty of places around here for that. I ain't no official swimmin' teacher, but I've been doin' it since I was five, and that's a good amount of time. But right now, we got to go get him."

There he was, standing next to the water's edge with a stick in one hand and a handlebar in the other, staring off into the distance like an old lady on the front porch waiting for her husband to come home.

"Elijah, get your butt outa here," I said as we got closer to him.

"I ain't doin' nothin' wrong. Just lookin' at a hole in the dirt what's filled with water."

"You just askin' for trouble, Elijah? You seen those signs all around here?

"What signs?"

"Geeze, maybe you can't swim, but I know you can read those signs. Is it you don't want to see'em?"

"Yea, I seen 'em."

"Me and Samson were talkin' about it. Swimmin', I mean. I'm gonna teach you. Now hop on your bike, and let's get out of here."

We hadn't gone too far down the path when the gunshots cracked the air. An old man came out from a cluster of kudzu-covered trees along the side of the road.

"Them was warnin' shots. They come once. Only once."

I wasn't sure if it was Peek at first because I'd always thought he'd be big. Big as Frankenstein. But he was a scrawny old man with torn overalls and a dirty red Peterbilt cap. His rifle pointed skyward, and he stared at us with eyes that could have been the bullets themselves, waiting their turn to fire. His skin looked white as chalk behind a gray stubble, and his lips had all but disappeared. He brought the rifle down and pointed it at us.

We stood there, Samson on one side of me, Elijah on the other, with Grover Peek no more than ten feet from us.

"This here's my property."

My chest was pounding so loud I wondered if any of them heard it. I looked into the face of the shriveled man and knew if any of us moved, we'd all be killed.

He looked at me. "I know who you are. I knew your sorry excuse of a pa." Then he shifted his eyes between Samson and Elijah as he spit some chaw juice. His focus came back to me. "What're you doin' with these two? I guess the nigger-lovin' apple don't fall too far now, ain't that right?"

Elijah's hands began to twitch. The old man pointed the gun barrel at him.

"Be still," I whispered, trying not to move my lips.

Fast as I said it, he jerked the gun back at me.

"Shut up, kid. You got that son-of-a-bitch's mouth. Never knowin' when to shut up or who to talk to." Sweat collected on his forehead and a drop of tobacco juice seeped from his mouth. "You know what he did, your no-good pa?"

"No, sir."

"He helped that scum-dog nigger boy escape before the trial."

I stood still, fixed in my shoes, not an eyelash moving.

"You know that?"

"No, sir, I don't know nothin' bout that, sir."

The old man spit again. He shook his head and blinked like his eyes had gone bad. He frowned and teetered for a minute. "He wouldn't never shut up 'bout the niggers havin' the same rights as us real Americans." Elijah twitched again, but Peek didn't see it. "The only right a nigger should have's the right to go back to Africa on a boat—in a pine box."

He shook his head and blinked again. "I fgrue yur tooooo rreaal . . ." It sounded like some foreign language. Then he collapsed to his knees.

The gun barrel kicked skyward as a shot went off. The bullet hit an upper branch of the oak beside us and ricocheted back down to the hard-packed soil. It skipped over Elijah's left foot and stopped. We scrambled out of the way. After the adrenalin settled, I looked at Grover Peek laid out in the dirt. One of his arms slapped the ground a couple times, like a hooked fish flapping against the shoreline. Then it stopped.

"Is he dead?" Samson said.

Elijah inched toward the old man. He picked up a stick and poked him in the stomach. I'd seen him do the same with dead jackrabbits. The old man's eyes opened.

Elijah jumped back. "Look," he yelled. "They movin'. They blinkin' and movin'."

Peek's eyes seemed to be the only part of him still alive, but they didn't look like bullets anymore. They looked like glossy blue marbles gliding back and forth. Then they blinked and blinked and blinked.

"Look there, he pissed his pants," Elijah said and poked him in the groin. A tear ran toward the old man's ear. Elijah poked him again.

"Stop doin' that," I said.

"Why?" He pointed the stick at Peek's eye.

"Stop," I yelled, looking around, feeling the weight of responsibility come over me. "This ain't right. I'm gonna get help."

I started to run toward home, then remembered Elijah's bike.

"Mama," I yelled at the top of my lungs all the way up our drive. "Mama, Mama, Grover Peek's dead." Her Skylark was nowhere to be seen. Uncle Mooks ran down the front steps.

"What'd you say?"

I dropped the bike to the ground. My lungs burned. "Grover Peek's dead, except for his eyes. Where's Mama? I need help."

Uncle Mooks laughed like I'd told him the

funniest joke he'd ever heard. "Hot damn." He moved his hips and did a stomping dance. "You sure?"

"Where's Mama?"

"Gone to town to deliver somethin'."

"I need her now," I screamed. "I need Mama."

Uncle Mooks laughed some more. "I say good riddance to bad rubbish."

"He ain't dead, dead. Just almost."

"Where?"

"On the ground by his pond."

He processed what I'd said and frowned. "What was you doin' there, on his land?"

"I need a hand, Uncle Mooks."

He made a sour face and shook his head. "Not my hand."

"Come on, you gotta," I whined.

"What was you doin' there, on his land?"

Quit askin' questions and help me."

"Why was you there?"

"Getting Elijah. Samson and Elijah's up there with him, now."

"Samson and Elijah? They ain't safe up there. No, it ain't safe." He paced, all the while looking at Elijah's bike lying in the yard.

He charged for the bike, picked it up, and pointed to the handlebars. "Get on."

His powerful legs pedaled us over exposed roots and jagged rocks. My butt bounced against the steel, and it took every bit of my strength to hang on. For all my life, I'd never seen Uncle Mooks venture off our property, and it surprised me when he took a shortcut I didn't know about.

Elijah stood guard, his trusty stick still pointed at the old man. Samson sat on a large rock, and watched.

Uncle Mooks spotted the gun on the ground. "He come after you boys?"

"Yessir, Mr. Mooks, he did." Elijah moved his stick in the direction of the bullet and then pointed it to the tree branch. "It hit that up there, then flew back and almost got me right here." He stuck out his foot.

"Sit with your brother," Uncle Mooks barked.

He picked up the rifle and turned his full attention to Grover Peek. He got down on his knees, leaned in close to his face, and looked into his watery blue eyes.

"I seen them eyes in my sleep for a long spell." He pointed the gun at Peek's head and raised his voice. "You know, they say time's a peculiar thing."

Peek's eyes fluttered.

Uncle Mooks looked up at me and yelled, "Ain't that what they say, Jason Lee?"

"I guess." I watched his finger on the trigger, ready to squeeze.

"I know some things 'bout time. Yep, I do. Don't

I, Jason Lee?"

I nodded, scared he'd pull the trigger and Peek's brains would fly out. But he kept on talking. "Let's say we was to drag you to the hospital so's you'd have a chance of gettin' fixed up good as new. Nope, we ain't gonna do that."

"Thought you was gonna help," I said.

"Told you I wouldn't." His eyes stayed fixed on Grover Peek. "He don't deserve it."

Uncle Mooks got up off his knees but kept the rifle pointed at Peek's head. He looked at Samson and Elijah.

"Let me tell you 'bout this old shit turd layin' on the ground. About what I seen him do. He strung up the young 'un from that tree over there."

The words came out so fast it wasn't until he nodded toward a chestnut oak halfway up a dusty hill that I understood. The tree had three naked branches poking out from the trunk.

"Let's say we was to string you up on that same tree?"

Peek's arm flapped once.

"We ain't gonna do that neither. Too much work. I'd rather stay put and watch you suck your last breath."

I felt like a bucket of cement had just dried on my chest. Samson and Elijah were still staring at the tree.

"I was a little boy hidin' in the shrubs that day,"

Uncle Mooks said. "Too scared to move. I watched the five of you string a rope around the boy's neck and hoist him." His face twisted and he wiped moisture from his eyes. "You know what they did after all the fight went outta him?"

I shook my head.

A blue vein popped out from his forehead. "They beat on him with baseball bats 'til there weren't nothin' left to hold him together." Uncle Mooks looked at the tree. "A kid the same age as me, no more than twelve."

Grover Peek's face was pure white. If I had to guess, I'd say mine looked the same.

Uncle Mooks kicked the old man in the ribs. "When it was over, you was the one who took his hood off. Four white-hooded boogie men and you, celebratin'."

He put his boot on Grover Peek's neck and pushed until the old man's throat rattled.

"Stop," I said. "Don't kill him."

"I already told you I ain't gonna do that."

The way things looked, I wasn't so sure.

"We're gonna watch for as long as it takes." Uncle Mooks lifted his boot off Peek's neck, walked to the rock, and sat between Samson and Elijah. The three of them seemed content to witness Grover Peek's life run out, no matter how long it took.

I yelled at them. "I'm gonna help him."

Uncle Mooks yelled back at me. "Help that old

shit turd? He kills kids, Jason Lee. Kids no different than you. Like I said before, he don't deserve it."

I had a mind to agree with him, but all I could see was the scar on the side of his head, deep as an empty eye socket.

I couldn't stop yelling. "It just ain't right, leavin' him here."

I looked at Samson and Elijah for backup and got none. They were steadfast as Uncle Mooks. Then, a flood of thoughts popped into my head. Things like lynchings and head wounds and fathers being killed in conflicts that they didn't have the balls to call wars and hate bigger than life or people.

"What's goin' on?"

Samson said nothing to me. Not even a grunt.

"You're actin' just like the old shit turd layin' there. You ain't actin' no better than him. I'm goin' for help. Real help this time."

I ran toward town, thinking back to what Mama had said about my daddy. "So almighty sure of what was right and wrong. And strong-willed enough to do the right thing when it went against everyone around him."

He had been a ghost of a man I'd only known from stories and photographs. At that minute, he was inside me, and I felt driven to do what I thought was right.

When I finally reached the road, my head pounding with a new strength not felt before, a pickup driving past gave me a ride. Like Uncle Mooks always said, fate carries its own clock.

Grover Peek didn't fare too well after his stroke. He suffered for two more years in The Sisters of Mercy Nursing Home. During that time, us boys used his pond as our own. Elijah learned to swim real good. Good as me.

The time finally came for us to watch as the procession of two cars and a hearse with Grover Peek's remains inside took the ride past our house from the Faith Deliverance Holy Church to the graveyard. Uncle Mooks watched from the couch as he cut up Fallstaff cans with his tin snips.

Sometimes I still get lost in the idea of what's right and what's wrong. It's not a simple thing.

The inspiration for the novel "The Clock Of Life" came from this story.

Cassie's Pond

Alcatraz had all but disappeared, smothered by a cloudbank working its way into the city. Propped up on pillows in my bay window, I watched the first tour boat of the morning heading toward it. The phone rang before the boat evaporated into the mist, and I picked up on the fifth ring.

"Cassie, this is June."

"I'm sorry, who?"

"I'm your Uncle Randy's wife." She spoke in a strong southern accent. "I know we've never met, but I'm calling to tell you he passed last month. He went peaceful. In his sleep."

"Uncle Randy? What happened?"

"Before his passing, he asked me to send you an old box from the upstairs storeroom."

"Did you say a month ago?"

"It's been up there all these years since Randy and I took over the place," she said at full speed. "It belonged to your Grandaddy. I'll be sending it tomorrow. That's what Randy wanted."

She hung up before I could say anything more. How did she get my phone number? How did she know where to send it?

The farmhouse was twenty miles outside Greensburg, Louisiana. I imagined her calling from the wall phone in the kitchen, with the long shallow sink and a floor full of spotted linoleum that dipped in front of the back door. The place had belonged to my dad's folks.

The year I turned seven, my dad drove away in his big Dodge truck with a woman whose hair looked like golden cotton candy. Despite his swift departure, my barely-a-kid-herself mom still dropped me off to spend summers there with Poppy, while she devoted those sultry days to the drifters she chased around with.

They roamed through the bayou country past marsh creeks and river levees. More often than not, they ended up in the never-sober city of New

Orleans. Her men hawked cleaning products and vacuum cleaners. One sharpened knives and mower blades out of the back of his converted station wagon.

Mom had times of rage that festered behind her steely eyes and erupted in rapid-fire, four-letter swear words. Those spells contrasted her angelic episodes. The dueling psyches were chronically at war with each other and with the men she needed like pain needs morphine.

Poppy's box arrived a week after June's phone call. At first glimpse, a flood of unplanned memories—whispers of a forgotten past—leaped from my senses in images from thirty years past.

I recalled a rope swing dangling like an intruder among weeping willow limbs. A shallow pond named for me, Cassie's Pond, was full of algae, but no fish. A cow named Moorene with jumping skin and a smile. I swear she smiled.

I ripped open the box. On top of all the papers was a dreadful yellow and brown photo of Pops and me. Uncle Randy's Instamatic had caught us off guard. We both looked toothless, seated in the dingy old armchair that stayed on the big porch for the better part of spring and summer. I was on his lap and the Magic Box sat on the wooden floor, next to his right leg.

Before Pops fetched it out of the dumpster

behind Mr. Benson's produce stand, it was only a cardboard okra carton. But slowly, over years, his ink-stained papers of stories and poetry had piled up inside. They grew into an inheritance of words shared with me, his blonde little Cassie. I'd run to him and ask, "Can we read from the Magic Box, Pops?"

I liked his names, Poppy and Pops. They felt good coming out of my mouth and bouncing off his big self, causing a smile.

"The box, Poppy, please?"

Off he'd go with loud, exaggerated footsteps, to fetch it. I'd crinkle my eyes and reach my small hands deep between the enchanting sheets. I'd rub my fingers across the pages to help me make my decision.

"This one. Read this one."

A big voice full of gravel and frogs and words that were pretty tumbled out from his mouth and fell on my shoulders, then slid down towards my lap as I tried to scoop them up with my hands to hold them forever.

> *Cobblestones --cobblewebs,*
> *Cobbles packed with my own dreads.*
> *Cobbled wishes -- wish I might.*
> *Please, my dear, no wishes tonight.*
> *I'll cobble wish -- if wish I want,*
> *And wish away this cobble haunt.*

I'll take each piece of cobbledense
And wish it makes some cobblesense.

Poppy smelled like warm arms in a flannel shirt weaved of coffee and pipe tobacco. He had skin the color of weather-beaten caramel and beryl green eyes that glistened under heavy lids. He wore messy shoes, like modern art, with spots and scuffs and streaks. He had gray hairs bursting out of his oversized ears. Strong ears for listening. I often tried to whisper low, invisible hiss-hiss words in those ears, but the hairs tickled my lips and made me laugh instead.

Uncle Randy laughed a lot too, with his extra big grin and red eyes in the morning. He wore blue uniform shirts that smelled like crawdaddys, with oblong patches over the pocket that said Randall. I remember thinking if he ever forgot it, he could simply look down to see his proper name, Randall.

His pants pockets bulged with Glassies and Moonies and Custards and Vaselines. I often found him playing marbles in the hard dirt behind the barn. He marked off the game circles with the round end of a tire pressure gauge. He cocked his thumb just so to take a shot. I'd hold my breath just before the quick tap when the steelie hit its target. Sometimes we played dominoes and go fish, but he was pretty much a marble expert back then, with three wooden cigar boxes chock full of Akro Agates to prove it.

He must have been about nineteen back then. The three of them, Pops, Nana, and Randy, drank liquor on the front porch late into the night. Out there, they laughed, barked cuss words at the world, stumbled, and slept like rag dolls propped up against the porch footstalls. Their black dog, named Dog, slept next to Nana. I'd watch them from the bedroom window until my eyelids got heavy and my head bobbed against the sill.

My initials were still on the top of the box, dug deep with his pocketknife. He had me carve them there, saying it proved that all the words inside were his *and* my words together.

The sheets inside have aged over the years, with faded script pressing against the frail, brittle papers. I found one that could have been about Dad, or Uncle Randy, or almost anyone in their family.

> *He walked through the dark with a stumble tumble.*
> *And drank from the flask with a humble rumble.*
> *His wrath came about with a mumble grumble.*
> *And only the night knew his bumble jumble*
> *The seasoned souse wouldn't fumble or crumble.*

Reading through the pages felt like secrets had been sent back to me to fill the hole that swallowed my childhood when Mom married Don. The week after the ceremony, on the morning of my tenth birthday, a wake-up call went off in the house that sounded like the birthday song and it looked like a cake with eleven candles—one to grow on. As fast as I blew them out, my world was taken away.

A twelve-foot U-Haul trailer hitched to Don's old four-door Chrysler was parked outside in our driveway, waiting to take me away. I stayed alone in the back seat while we drove west for five days. We stopped off the main road only once, to see a ghost town named Jerome, Arizona, then headed straight for San Jose, California.

Don sold Watkins products and wore wrinkled brown suits, even on the trip out west. He called me Casandra, because nicknames were for pets and babies, not young ladies. In the time it took him to say it, my name changed from Cassie Ballard to Casandra DuBois. Soon after Don's "in name only" adoption of me, mom's menacing voice warned me to never speak of my father's family again.

About six months after we arrived in California, Mom tiptoed into my room one night and whispered a nightmare in my ear. She said Poppy had died and gone to heaven with the angels. She patted my back, walked out of my room, and never mentioned him again.

Each night for the next year, I went to bed wondering if, because I went away, his heart had grown so heavy from sorrow it splintered into a million pieces. I might have killed him.

Don made mom happy until the day she changed her mind. Then the two of us moved to Noe Street in San Francisco, and I entered my third friendless school since we'd left Louisiana.

The kids had already paired up with their best friends, so I spent my time alone on the stoop, available should someone come by who wanted to play. I wrote stories on thin onionskin papers, placed them in my own cardboard carton, and waited for them to grow and steep and turn to magic.

My quick-change-artist mother learned the city ways well. Like a skilled ventriloquist, her Louisiana drawl disappeared, a quirky kind of grace surfaced, and the cussing ceased.

She changed her name to Suzanne and carried a small month-at-a-glance calendar to record her dates. Suzanne found a different class of salesmen with expense accounts. They traveled to the West Coast for sales meetings, and they wore wedding bands.

She lived for them and dated often. Bobby sox cute, small and pert, she dressed in pastel sweaters and pencil skirts, slit up the back. She wore little makeup, which produced an exterior of innocence.

Like the heroine of the movie *The Three Faces Of Eve* she could be demure and retiring, then rowdy and irresponsible, or eccentric and exotic. When confronted with the word *no*, Suzanne became plain old mean.

She had worked her way up at Macy's, from the first floor costume jewelry department to fourth-floor fine accessories, specializing in handbags that cost three times her weekly take-home pay. A view of the gentler crowd settled mom down, and she swore off men for close to two years. We spent her free time together exploring our new city, as pretend sisters.

"One adult and a child's ticket for my little sister," she'd say.

We hopped on trolleys that clanged up steep hills past exotic Chinatown and clipped, arm-in-arm, past noisy sea lions by The Wharf. We hiked up Telegraph Hill to catch the view, puffing with each step.

My favorite street, Lombard, zigged and zagged as though it had been built for a Keystone Kop's movie. We, just us two sisters, shared the city together until my first year of high school when Suzanne met Robert, a Chiropractor who lived in a large house near Walnut Creek.

I have grown to know San Francisco like a native, but thirty years and a past of unspoken secrets had eroded memories of Louisiana. Pops' papers shook them loose.

Things came back to me dreamlike. I couldn't remember Poppy working the farm—only being with me. Every morning, he combed my ashy hair into pigtails and tied red ribbons around them. I could have done it myself, but we both liked it better when he did it.

Nana frowned a lot and didn't have much to say to anyone. She shuffled around in house slippers and listened to music on an old radio with brown knobs. Every Monday, she made big breakfasts of fried cornmeal and Karo Syrup and then cooked up a pot of red beans and rice for supper.

Early on those summer mornings, before the smell of coffee, I could find Poppy at the kitchen table writing his poetry. He let me stay if I was "Quiet as the leaves dropping from a tree in the next county." I sat on the slanted floor, underneath the table, next to his messy shoes, and scratched out my own words on newspaper with crayons.

My condo soon became a place where I wanted to be, with his box perched on the kitchen table. Next to it, I spread stacks of his papers and mingled them with rough drafts of my work. The heart-warming bundles filled my stark, contemporary life. They felt like notes pinned to my jumper, reminding me where I came from.

Even though I had learned at an early age that the past and the relatives whose blood whisked and whirled inside me were off limits, the papers validated that the distant longings I felt flittering somewhere in darkness all those years were not just made up.

> *Cassie's dreams flutter about*
> *Like frantic moths.*
> *They touch all parts of her soul*
> *And leave their meaning just out of reach.*
> *Drowsily welcoming the morning,*
> *Her senses remember the visit,*
> *And somehow, it makes daylight a little brighter.*
> *Her body is ready for the new day,*
> *….and totally unaware of*
>   *the four-winged, night-flying insect*
>   *desperately trying to escape*
>   *through the solid glass window.*

I'd advanced in income and status over the years with a successful court reporting business. I wasn't so lucky with personal connections. Men watched me turn from velvet to stone in quaint, romantic situations. At their first attempt to get close, I imagined seeds of desertion germinating and studied every eyebrow quiver and forehead spasm for wrinkles of disapproval. Then, when they finally walked out on me, bloodied from my barbed wire shield, I felt deserving of abandonment.

Suzanne stopped by a year ago, looking like Debbie Reynolds doing an impression of Bette Davis. My mother, who had vanished from my life without a phone call, a Christmas card, or a "Good-bye, I'm-leaving, no-need-to-worry," darted around my condo. She wore a black felt cape and an old-fashioned, veiled pillbox hat. A mother-of-pearl cigarette holder was clamped between two of her fingers.

I stood there dumb-struck as an idiot child. A foghorn blew somewhere off in the bay. Detachment seemed second nature, taught to me by the woman flapping about before me.

With an affected tone, she explained how she and Victor Somebody, a retired veterinarian, were in Palm Springs during the season and Laguna Beach for summers. Then she said, "I thought we'd have an evening together, just the two of us, like we used to. I bought tickets to the theater. Want to go?" She smiled.

I heard, *"One adult and a child's ticket for my little sister."*

"Thanks, but no," I said nervously. "I'm working on a book and plan to spend the evening writing. Uncle Randy's wife sent me Poppy's Magic Box." It was the first time I ever said *no* to her.

Her face turned pale and tight.

"I'm putting his papers together with the stuff I've written over the years. That's what all this mess is, the papers stacked up here."

We looked at each other through a dreadful silence. My head began to pound, and I involuntarily slipped back into my childhood for a moment. *Fishing on Cassie's pond, a dog named Dog, and marbles with Uncle Randy.*

"Did know Uncle Randy died?"

"Uncle Randy, who?" she said. "Magic Box?" Her lip twitched.

I glanced out the window, and then back into her steely eyes. She laughed at me and walked to the table. Then she grabbed a fist full of pages and threw them on the floor, her felt cape billowing.

"Don't ever bring up that family in front of me. You've always known, even as a little girl, not to mention *those* people. I pulled you off that farm. How dare you turn me down to stay home with some filthy pieces of paper."

Paralyzed by her wrath, I watched as she picked up another handful of papers. She pulled a lighter out of the cape pocket and set fire to them.

"No, no, no, no, no," I kept saying, but I couldn't move. My body turned stiff as a porcelain figurine. "No, no, please no," I moaned and noticed that behind the shadows of her veiled hat, the flame's reflection lit her wild eyes.

She reached for the papers on the floor and ripped them as her cape wrapped around her body in a shroud of treachery, all in slow motion.

I smothered the fire with a potholder as that woman named Suzanne bolted out my front door. The slam took a while to reach me. It shattered my stony armor, and I felt something happening through a long, long silence.

The ink from Poppy's skillful pen melted into silent blue tears. They flowed up from the bottom of my toes and escaped through my eyes. The living room reshaped itself around me, into a cool, damp well, like in storybooks, with a small, pointed roof.

Inside the well, I found a bucket crowded with charred flesh, and heart, and words on onionskin, attached to a frayed rope. I rummaged through the debris and captured the pieces of paper, smeared and unreadable.

Poppy's soft hand patted my head, and he read all of them for me long into the night. And gravel, and frogs, and words that were pretty tumbled out from my memory fell on my shoulders, then slid down towards my lap as I tried to scoop them up with my computer to hold them forever.

Morning drops on spider webs
spin song without an ear
in attics bare of memory
left empty through the year

As winds touch weeds and left debris
in danceless cabaret

the future smiles with earnest triste
'cause time has gone astray

It's taken some time, but our book, Pops' and mine, has been published. It's titled Cassie's Pond, and the dedication reads, "With the love of my childhood to Poppy Ballard."

His ninety-fourth birthday would have been the same day as my first book signing.

Chapter One. I had a willow pole with a small bell attached to the top that was supposed to ring when a fish nibbled, but it didn't. I never caught a fish in Cassie's Pond and never saw anyone else catch one.

Garage Sale Confidential

Liz died in 2010. Cancer.

I stumbled across the letter yesterday, while shuffling through a drawer. Her letter. The sight of it transported me back almost twenty years, to the moment she handed it to me.

Arthur watched television in the den while Liz and I worked in the garage. We still had dozens of boxes to sift through before the weekend sale. Liz scribbled prices on orange sticky dots, and I stuck them on the various china platters, the discarded crock pots, exercise equipment, and the toys that hadn't been played with for years.

She glanced toward the door into her house.

"Trina," she said in a low voice, then passed me an envelope. "I can't throw this away. Will you save it for me?" Her eyes held steady on mine. "It's confidential."

"Sure."

I burned with curiosity while studying the dog-eared envelope. The sender had used a bold felt-tip pen, the writing precise, like that of someone who does things well. With obedient loyalty I folded the envelope and slipped it into my back pocket.

Liz and Arthur were moving to a gated community after years of living in their once ideal neighborhood. Wrought-iron bars on neighbor's windows had become more prevalent, and home-security signs now peppered the lawns.

The scuff of Arthur's slippers against the cement floor announced his arrival. The bypass surgery had shrunk his interest in life. A heavy sigh launched his sentence. "How're you gals getting along?"

"We're getting there," Liz said. "It would go faster if we had another pair of hands. Manly hands."

Arthur almost smiled.

I'd been a bridesmaid at their wedding but could barely remember that Arthur—the one with vibrant eyes and a boyish gusto for life.

His heavy eyes scanned the utility table covered with kitchenware. He picked up one of the Ziggy mugs, *ten cents each.*

"You're selling these? Why? They're nice."

"There are only three of them. They're stupid, and who wants to drink out of a Ziggy mug anyway?" Liz said.

"Why don't we keep 'em? Maybe the missing one'll show up in another box."

"Fine, I'll set them aside. If I find the fourth one—"

Arthur rescued the three by nestling them in the safety of his flannel shirt. "I'll take them in the house with me, just in case. The game's probably back on."

When he closed the door behind him, Liz said, "He wants to keep everything."

She tore into a carton of hand-carved nativity figurines. I stayed quiet. We'd been friends for years. With that kind of time comes an undeclared acceptance of each other. Liz was an exotic species with the ability to cause dazzling turbulence, and I was the dutiful friend.

We met in college, in an off-the-wall class called, "The Art of Sin and the Sin of Art." The course catalog said, "Lust with the saints and burn with the sinners." I was there to burn through an easy A. Liz's reason had more to do with sinning, and the new professor.

The friendship happened as fast as a collision. I admired the way she took risks and favored behavior that tested boundaries. And I prized that she shared it all with me, her quiet, less-than-adventurous new friend. She gave me acceptance, a most precious thing.

She removed three porcelain wise men, *three for a dollar*, from sheets of newspaper.

"Listen to me saying he wants to keep everything after I stuck you with that envelope." She shook her head the way you do when you need thoughts to leave.

"No problem. Your secret's mine."

"I know."

She gave me her what-the-fuck-am-I-doing look, then plopped down on a wobbly bentwood chair, *three dollars*. She had pulled her thin bangs to the side and secured them with bobby pins as though she was about to wash her face. The dim lighting veiled her soft beauty and darkened her eye sockets. She said, "I thought I could handle this alone, but it's sucking me dry like an insidious leech."

"Yuck."

"Yuck is right." She studied a crack in the concrete. "Turns out, that old need for outside approval from men is still with me." She looked up. "This one's a pisser, Trina. Different from when we were younger and I did all that, well, you remember, exploring my earthy side."

I nodded, considering her understatement.

The chair squealed as she stood up, looked around, and sat right back down.

"Get it off your chest. It's me." I waited for her to come clean about the mysterious envelope tucked next to my ass.

"You know I stayed content being faithful to Arthur for a long stretch."

"Yes, I know that. Then what happened?"

"Last September, I went to my forty-fifth reunion. High school."

"With Arthur?"

"No. He doesn't go to those things anymore."

"He doesn't do much, does he?"

She talked over my words. "I bumped into an old friend of mine, Rob."

"I don't recall ever hearing about a Rob." I made finger quotes as I said his name.

"High school, before I met you. He was a guy friend. I don't know why we never dated. We should have."

"Everyone has someone like that," I said.

"College sent us in different directions."

"College, Smollege, let's fast forward to this September."

"Thought you'd like some background."

"Nope. September."

"Okay, okay. I felt disconnected at the reunion, and alone. I read nametags and smiled at people I didn't recognize, and I recognized people who didn't remember me. At some point, it hit me that I was older than my parents had been at the time of my graduation. That got me spinning with emotion, and ticked-off at Arthur for staying home."

"That's one for a shrink."

"Then Rob walked up with a grin and a hug. He instantly took me back to the place where troubles were little more than deciding what to wear that day."

"Married? Single? What?"

"He came alone."

"Alone meaning not married?"

"Not exactly alone, he came with Sam Cooperman, his best friend from school. We used to call him Coop."

"So, he's married, and you don't want to say it."

"Let me tell my story."

Liz started to build, as was our pattern. Over the years, our friendship strengthened whenever she talked about her reckless, back-alley misbehaviors. These uncensored times were as confidential as a Swiss bank account, and as complex as a dark, pungent fragrance that would certainly repel others.

She smiled and closed her eyes. "I hadn't seen Rob since graduation. The years were good to him.

He stood out. His Italian suit hung soft, maybe an Armani. Dark hair, maybe Grecian Formula. But his eyes." She paused. "They'd turned reflective. Alluring. We spent the whole evening together until three in the morning."

"I'm all ears."

She pulled the bobby pins from her bangs and unconsciously coaxed the hair to rest on her forehead. A few stayed up.

"That night, all my old needs crept out. Hell, they leapt out. Especially the need for mischief and danger and the ritual of being taken again."

"Liz, you're almost swooning. The sex, was it mischievous or dangerous?"

"We didn't have a chance. That damn Coop caught up with us whenever we strolled out of sight. "

"That wouldn't have happened in the good old days."

"Would you like me to continue?"

"Sorry, never mind. Go on."

"About a week later, he sent me a letter. A steamy, suggestive, stream-of-conscious thing. I read it and read it and walked around in an erotic excitement that got in the way of everything."

"Is that what you gave me?"

"No. I threw the first one away. I gave you the second letter." Her foot bounced. "In the meantime, we phoned each other constantly, horny as teenagers, planning when we could get together. I wish I'd kept that first letter so you could understand what I went through."

As Liz stood, the bentwood chair squealed again. "Maybe you should just read it. You'll get the idea, and save me a lot of explaining. There's wine in the kitchen. I'll pour us some."

"You want me to read it now? What if Arthur comes out again?"

"I'll be in there with him. Don't worry. Back in a few."

I pulled the envelope out of my pocket, opened the gummy flap, and took out the letter. He typed the whole thing in italics. It was dated December 13th, 1993. I wondered if it had been a Friday.

My initial plan—to be an impartial, uninvolved voyeur.

Dear Elizabeth, Good god you called!

I thought for sure that my inept first stab at a letter had put you off. Perhaps I came across as a pedant. I'm not that cerebral. Ok, maybe competitive and superficial, but pedantic, never!

My mind raced after our time together. I fantasized fifteen different scenarios, and none of them included Sam Cooperman. The subtle, sexual undercurrent to our conversations helped with the fantasies. Even though living with perpetually rutting teenagers may have warped my perception, I definitely feel a sensual ground spring in our intercourse (see).

I'm looking forward to seeing you…that's a small understatement…like a seven year old looking forward to his first trip to Disneyland. Every time I think about you I get this really wicked grin on my face. I sit here smiling and shaking my head from side to side. I don't know exactly what it is I'm looking forward to. Might it be fantasyland? adventureland? tomorrowland? incarceration in a scummy Mexican jail?

I stopped reading and went over to the stationary bike, *twenty-five dollars*, and straddled the seat. A rusted sled hung from the rafters above my head, *make offer.*

My jaw tightened. Envy and irritation struck. Who was this guy? Why couldn't I have met him? Or, if not him, someone enthralled enough to write to me like that?

Pathetic, I thought. I'm single, divorced for six years, with no dates to talk about, and here I am riding a stationary bike next to a card table stacked with porcelain elephants, *fifty cents each,* and a Karaoke machine, *fifteen dollars, never used.* As usual, whatever Liz was going through seemed preferable.

I needed to sort out my feelings before she came back from the house, but instead, my thoughts turned to the two of them at their reunion, stirring up a roomful of gossip. I imagined them slow dancing, and heard the music. *'Are the stars out tonight? I don't know if it's cloudy or bright, 'cause I only have eyes for you.'* Liz glances up to see Rob smile at her.

Then I got back to the letter.

I thought about you many times over the last four decades. I thought about you during bad times, like when I tried to create a world of sanity in the midst of all the stink and the rot of the Vietnam jungle. I thought about you during the good times, too. Over the years you have never been far from my thoughts. You have always been there, reminiscent of the famous Columbia Pictures torchbearer—a shining, beautiful beacon of my youth.

"What are you reading?" Arthur asked.

"Shit." I jumped and looked up.

"Oh, sorry."

"You startled me." The words came out uneven and shrill. I folded the letter. "Notes for an early meeting tomorrow."

Over the years, by default, I'd been peripherally involved in conspiracies against Arthur. I served as Liz's alibi for some of her indiscretions, and provided the hideaway for others. But there, in his cold, quiet garage, with another man's letter stinging my hand, I wanted to apologize.

Arthur looked around. I pedaled casually,

grateful for the whirling sound, and finally said, "It must be hard for you – getting rid of all these memories."

"No." He scanned the tables. "Memories can never go away, no matter how many crock-pots you sell." His voice seemed hollow. "There are nights I lie in bed next to Liz and marvel at all the things we've been through and shared." He stopped and looked at me. "I know that sounds corny. I've turned sappy since my operation."

His fingers caressed the etched neck of a purple bud vase, *two dollars*. "I don't remember this. It's nice." He picked it up. "Sorry, I'm no help. I've got the flu or something."

"Where's Liz?" I asked. "She went to get wine but never came back."

"She's on the phone. Kyle called. It'll probably be awhile."

Their sons had married and moved on.

"Where's Kyle now? Chicago?"

Arthur nodded.

On the way back to the house, he said, "Kevin's in Grand Junction."

Friendships are delicate threads that sometimes tangle, and sometimes pull taught. At that moment, I wanted to leave and have nothing to do with Liz anymore. But I stayed. She needed me.

I smoothed the letter out on the handlebars. A part of me wished that Arthur would come back and see it.

You liked me, accepted me, made me feel worthwhile. There have been many others since you, but you were a keystone to my worldly education.

The idea of first love (yes, yes I admit it) is so powerful that seeing you again, remarkably beautiful and as strong as I always remembered, has consumed me with thoughts of fulfilling my boyhood obsession to be with you.

The bike grew harder to pedal, then shuddered to a stop. I wondered if I'd ever made that kind of an impact on anyone. Made anyone feel that good and accepted? Made anyone feel worthwhile? I must have. But how would I know?

14 December (I'm back. Couldn't finish this letter yesterday, too many interruptions)

I've learned a lot over the past thirty years. Eleven months and fourteen days in that green hell where I lost my youth; four years of college where I discovered my humanity; six or seven legit careers where I built real world experience; two marriages where I learned I enjoyed having a date every Friday and Saturday night; friendships made, cultivated, savored; friendships neglected and lost. My decisions, the paths I followed, are paved with all these.

Being with you for an evening, after such a long hiatus, sparked a burning compulsion to fill in the missing pages of our personal histories. I'm even working out these days, hard. I want to look like my old self for you.

I want to know about everything you've done and thought since our shared days of innocence. I want to tell you about all my triumphs; my disappointments. The years have indelibly marked our bodies and our souls with who we were and what we've become.

Liz came back carrying a wedge of Brie and a bottle of Merlot. She set the cheese on a wooden cutting board, *twenty-five cents*, and poured the wine into heavy pottery goblets with sculpted troll faces. "Hippie glasses," she said and laughed. "I made them myself. What do you think? Fifty cents?"

"I can't believe you left me here all alone with this letter," I snapped. "Shit, Arthur came out and caught me reading it."

"Did you finish?"

"Did I finish?" I said, very put out. "No. I got as far as his burning compulsion to hash over your days of innocence and then share your marked bodies."

"Meow," she said. "You might as well finish it. I'll wait."

"Don't even think of leaving again."

As I said at the reunion, I resigned from P.T.S. and sold my interest in the consulting firm last month. I figure it's time to limit my commitments and start living a normal person's life, doing a sixty-hour week instead of an eighty-four. Hell, I'm going to be the father of a newborn within a couple of weeks. By the way, Liz, for names, we've picked Thomas Patrick if it's a boy and Elizabeth if it's a girl.

I'm tired and worn out. I don't need this newborn baby routine...I've already done that...years ago! Eeaaaaah!!...I must be out of my mind.

Well enough playing around. It's time to post this letter.

I need to see you!

Love, Rob

I didn't want to talk to her, and pretended to still be reading a while longer. A jolt of spite shot through my chest, along with an immediate need to protect Rob from her. So much for my impartial voyeur idea.

One time she and I took a weekend trip to Vegas, and she spent the night with a craps dealer. The following day, I asked, "Why him?"

"I don't know. He was fun, and he was there. It's sort of like going on an eating binge. A fleshy, primal craving kicks in, and all I can do is feed it."

I expected her to say something along the same line when I set the letter in my lap.

"Okay, I'm done."

A bead of red wine dripped down the grotesque

face of the troll goblet in her hand. Her brows pinched as if a pain struck, and tears fell.

"What's wrong?"

"He's dead," she said.

My skin erupted with chill bumps. Her mouth moved, but I missed some of the words.

"...I walked around, fueled by anticipation so strong it sometimes caused me to stop cold. I couldn't shake the delicious, bad girl thing. I called him the day I got that letter, and we planned to meet the next day." She glanced toward the door to the house. "It stormed like a mother all day, but that wasn't going to stop me."

I adjusted myself on the bike seat, preparing for the *'he's dead'* part of the story.

"A big rig had jackknifed, and traffic didn't budge, for hours." She took a sip of wine. "My cell phone went dead. You should have seen me. I cursed the weather and screamed at all the hopped-up truck drivers in the world. I was a sexually frustrated, freaked-out crazy woman, going nowhere, except possibly straight to hell for wanting Rob so bad. "

"Was he in the accident?

"What?"

"You said he died."

"No, no, no. Not there."

"Jesus, Liz, what happened? What happened to Rob?" I almost yelled it.

She looked at me as if trying to recapture a dream. "The next day, Coop called me. Rob had told him about us. He said that Rob went to the gym before leaving to meet me. He had a heart attack while working-out on the rowing machine."

"Oh, Liz."

"I wanted to smell him, feel his smoothness, his hardness."

"Liz, don't do this to yourself."

"Part of me misses him as if we'd been having an affair for all those years. Another part wants to hover over Arthur every minute and apologize for being consumed with a dead man."

She wiped her eyes with the tips of her fingers, turned around, and returned to pricing the nativity sets and stray figurines.

I got off the bike to hug her. She held a carved baby in a manger, *twenty-five cents*. As my arms wrapped around her, she said in a whisper, "Coop told me Rob's wife went into labor the next day and had a little girl."

We stayed wrapped together until Liz pulled away with a nod of gratitude. I went back to work in the quiet of her sadness.

"Look, Trina."

I turned to see the fourth Ziggy mug, *ten cents*, in her hand.

"Arthur would be glad this turned up. Too bad it's broken," she said, letting it drop to the concrete.

Her Spittin' Image

They found Aunt Loretta's last will and testament on her nightstand, scribbled on a Chinese menu from her favorite takeout, Mr. Chow's.

In blue ink, over the featured specials, Moo Goo Gai Pan and Pressed Duck, she had written, "I bestow my clothes, furniture, and all the items left in my apartment, on the Salvation Army." That's what she wrote—bestow.

At the bottom of the menu, below the list of desserts—green tea ice cream, coconut balls, and lychee—she wrote, "I bequeath my beloved Fenry to my niece, Miranda Tillman, with the stipulation that she take at least one road trip with him. After that, his fate is up to her."

The news of her death and my odd inheritance came just before my eighteenth birthday. I had been busy counting the days until summer's end, anxious for my classes at Cornell to begin.

Because of my lifelong infatuation for Aunt Loretta, I found her intentions weirdly sweet, but her "beloved" Fenry just happened to be a thirty-four year old Honda Civic that smelled like an old set of dentures wrapped in a moldy shirt. His full name was Fenry Honda, named, of course, after the old movie star. I knew how much Aunt Loretta loved that car, but my parents had just bought me a brand-new Beemer. The sheer idea of owning Fenry filled me with a private disappointment.

Why couldn't she have left me a more practical keepsake, like a necklace or a prized memento from one of the many trips she had taken? Better yet, why couldn't she have, just once, taken me with her when she was still here?

She didn't visit us often, but when she did, I was drawn to her the way a flower seeks the sun. We looked alike, each spared the thick Tillman ankles and the only ones splattered with freckles that spread, as Aunt Loretta liked to say, from hell to breakfast, all over our skin. She and I were the only redheads in the family, and I loved to touch her long braid that tumbled to her waist.

Aunt Loretta knew things no other Tillman knew. Things like origami, and how to read tea leaves, and play the bagpipes. I wanted her to teach those things to me, her little look-alike.

Before she got leukemia, or, as she called it, "the curse of the living L," she craved adventure and set out to see everything she could. She traveled the backroads, slept outdoors, and crisscrossed America. Aunt Loretta carried an energy of spirit into any room. That's what I wanted to inherit from her the most.

The awkward part was that everyone else in the Tillman family did their best to avoid her, especially my parents. On more than one occasion, when my mother thought I'd gone to my room, I heard her spew her disapproval. *"Free spirit, my ass. Lost soul's more like it. . .wild. . . selfish."*

Her loathing ran deep. I wondered why my father let her say those things about his only sister, even though I knew Aunt Loretta's bohemian ways didn't blend well with my mother's conventional tastes.

I didn't have siblings, so as a kid, I invented friends. We played tea parties and whispered secrets. One time, my make-believe friends were my dad and Aunt Loretta when they were kids. The pretend boy who played my dad stood tall and lanky as a beanpole and didn't have a speck of dirt on him. He rapped his knuckles on the picnic table to get our attention, and then he told us, the two red-headed little girls, that we were going to play bank. We ran, hand in hand, as fast as we could to escape to my room. Instead of playing bank, we fed the stuffed bears and lions before wheeling them off in my wagon for their performances in the circus.

As the planets align in mysterious ways, her funeral, the first one I'd ever attended, took place on the morning of my eighteenth birthday.

We, the assorted branches of the Tillman family tree, caravanned to the mortuary in limousines. I sat on the backseat with my legs stretched out, and kept busy by picking the polish off my nails. Dad sat facing me, close to the small bar provided. He scribbled a last-minute eulogy on two of the complimentary cocktail napkins fanned out next to the liquor carafes.

"That's just rude," I said, chipping away at a thumbnail. He didn't hear me.

We pulled into the parking lot. The smell of freshly paved tar lingered in the air. The minister waited for us next to his car. We huddled around him, making somber conversation about the chance of a summer storm. I stepped outside the circle. Talking about the weather before a funeral felt vulgar.

Six motorcycles with ear-piercing exhaust's

rumbled into the lot. The riders lined the bikes up, back side to the curb. Then, as though overrun by an impromptu parade, a stream of colorful, late-model vans and trucks entered the lot, bearing license plates from all parts of the country.

We Tillmans, all respectfully clothed in black, stood by the limousines and watched as the people emerged from their vehicles. They milled, forming a colorful sea of Hawaiian prints and flamboyant clothes that rippled in the summer wind. They all knew each other. They were loud—and joyful.

"For the love of God," my mother said to the minister. "Can we do something about these people?"

A woman in a chartreuse caftan and matching turban shuffled geisha-style, quickly toward us.

"Loretta?" she said to me, then stopped and brought her hand to her forehead. "My God, what's wrong with me? I'm in shock. You're her spittin' image."

The intensity of her reaction set me back, as Aunt Loretta would say, all the way to last Thursday.

"I'm so sorry. You must be her daughter."

While my mouth politely said, "I'm Miranda, Loretta's niece," my head thought, wouldn't it be cool to pretend to be her daughter for the day? Only one day, for these strangers. The idea didn't seem ridiculous at all but rather tempting.

My mother rushed over to pick pretend lint off my jacket, her smile tight, her eyes fixed on the woman's chartreuse crown.

"Time we go in, dear." She locked her hand around the back of my arm and steered me toward the funeral hall. "It's best you don't speak to these people," she said in a hushed, low directive.

We weren't close, my folks and I. For them, careers took center stage. I used to wonder, and still do, if they ever wanted to scoop me up in their arms, hug me, and smell my hair or if they felt those tasks were more suited to the nannies.

By the time I turned fourteen, the course they had mapped out for me was as precise as a to-do list.

One: College degree from Cornell, my mother's alma mater.

Two: Masters from my dad's old ivied halls, Dartmouth.

Three: Career at a prestigious financial institute. Four: Success.

A short list. No five or six. No space for edits.

I looked back at the woman in chartreuse, shrugged my shoulders, and waved goodbye. Walking up the steps of the funeral parlor, I didn't know what to expect inside. A kind-looking man ushered my mother and me past several people already seated. We took a spot in the first row. My chest tightened, and my breath became shallow when I realized the coffin placed on the platform was open.

It didn't take long before a lack of oxygen transformed all my rational thoughts into an out-of-body episode. How else could I explain myself floating, hovering in the rafters above the ceremony? And I saw myself, small and drab, in the front pew below, clueless and uneasy.

After floating for a while I straddled a beam and held it tight until the service started. A bearded man went to the lectern. His orange tee shirt said, *Biketoberfest, Daytona Beach, 2000*. His voice boomed through the microphone as he spoke of the first time he met my Aunt Loretta near Cathedral Rock in Sedona.

She had sent me a postcard from there and most every other place she'd been. My mother bristled each time one arrived and didn't know I kept all of them, one hundred and forty-three, in a Jimmy Choo shoe box under my bed. Sometimes, Aunt Loretta sent me snapshots. I had thirty-seven. She had drawn an arrow on each one that pointed toward her head. Next to the arrow, she wrote, "I am here." I would look at them and think, "Oh, there you are, my missing aunt. I'm here, waiting for you to take me with you."

One time, she and Fenry drove for days just to see the largest ball of twine in Cawker, Kansas, and then dashed off to Washington, D.C., because a "stinky plant" bloomed for the first time in ten years. Her worn-out duffel bags were always packed and waiting in Fenry's back seat, ready for the next spur-of-the-moment journey. One duffle held clothes and essentials, and the other was packed with tools and spare parts.

From my position in the rafters, Aunt Loretta looked pleased inside the casket, even though her face was waxen. The corners of her mouth turned up, and a dusty rose gloss stained her lips. She wore a white kimono. Her hair was free from the braid and cascaded over her shoulders like it had been placed there by a master artist.

The woman from the parking lot, the one in chartreuse, took the lectern and talked about their yearly trips to Carlsbad Caverns for the reading of tarot cards and some kind of candle spells. Then each of the strangers in attendance stood and spoke, sharing their memories of her.

I looked back to the casket. Aunt Loretta's eyes opened, and as quick as a thought, she appeared on the rafter next to me.

"It's nice up here, isn't it?" she said.

I held on tight and nodded.

"So, what's on your mind, Miranda?"

I whispered, not to disturb the services. "Aunt Loretta? There's something I've always wanted to ask you."

"You'd better hurry," she whispered back.

"Sometimes at night, when I looked at the pictures you sent me, I dreamed myself there, accepted by you and the others. Everyone's arms wrapped around me as though I was special. And then, when morning came, I wondered why you never asked me to go with you."

"Miranda, you are special."

I looked at her waxy face and believed her.

"But why didn't you ever take me along?"

Aunt Loretta dropped heavy as a stone back into her casket. The only sound I heard came from my pounding heart. She must have heard it, too, because she smiled at me and said, "Pay attention to that heart, Miranda, and take good care of Fenry. He'll help you find your own adventures."

I adjusted my weight and looked down to where my father sat. His face shined like wet plastic. His shoulders slumped as though his bones had gone limp. The eulogy cocktail napkins dangled from his right hand. He brought one of them to his forehead, patted twice, and tucked it into his breast pocket.

And then I was back at my place on the bench, seated next to my mother, looking up at the empty beams. I couldn't trust myself to understand anything. I wanted my mother to take my hand or stroke my face. I'd felt that way many times, but that day, it finally sunk in that she simply couldn't be there for me, and I had to let go of the notion.

Because of the rafters incident, as the days passed, I became more eager to pick up Fenry and keep him as my own. *Pay attention to your heart, Miranda, and take good care of Fenry*, she had said from her casket. Somehow, he might help me listen to my heart.

I found my mother in the den reading the *National Review*.

"Are you busy?" I asked, startling her.

"Not really." She set the magazine down.

The afternoon light spilled through the shutters and cast rigid shadows on the back wall and across her face.

"I'd like to get Fenry today. Will you go with me and drive the Beemer back?"

Her face pinched as if she'd been struck by a sharp head pain. "Miranda, you're not to bring that piece of junk here. We'll donate it."

"What?"

"You heard me."

Her tone snapped my mood to defiance. "I'm going to keep him," I said, loud.

She stood and clamped my hands onto her hips, elbows cocked. "You can't keep it. I won't allow it."

"Watch me."

My mother grabbed my arm. Her fingers

pressed to the bone. "I'll say it again. That piece of junk's not welcome here."

I wrenched my arm from her. She reached for me again. Her face came close.

"You're hurting me."

"You will not keep that car." Each word came out like a mallet hitting a tom-tom. "You will not keep that car," she said, again then again.

"What's going on?" I took a step back and rubbed my arm.

"I'm the one who raised you."

"Have you gone insane? What's that got to do with getting Fenry?"

"I raised you."

"If you want to get technical, the nannies raised me."

Her pupils expanded. "She's dead. Your Aunt Loretta's dead."

"Yes, she is. I know. And she bequeathed me her car. His name is Fenry Honda. I'm going to keep him. I'll get someone else to help me."

My mother clutched the air in frustration. "She promised to stay away."

"What's going on? You're scaring me."

I'd love to say she put her arms around me and we sat on the couch holding each other, but instead, she pointed her polished index finger at me.

"That selfish bitch is still doing it."

"Okay, I give up. You've always been jealous of

Aunt Loretta, and that's what this is about."

"She doesn't deserve your love," she screamed. "She gave birth to you, then planned to adopt you out." Her voice cracked with rage. "It was us, your father and I, who gave you everything."

I couldn't have been more crushed if an elephant had sat on me. She kept talking, but I couldn't catch all the words.

"Birth mother. . . free spirit. . . ran from responsibility. Lifestyle. . .wild. . .selfish."

I tried to say stop, but nothing came.

"She begged your father and me to adopt you."

I held my breath as I tumbled down the steep facade of my life. My heart pumped blood through my body against my will.

Finally, it came.

"STOP."

Her voice lowered. "We didn't tell you because the three of us agreed that no one else should ever know." She put both hands to her forehead. "I'm sorry."

The words pulsed through my head. *I'm sorry, I'm sorry, I'm sorry.* But I couldn't tell *who* was sorry. My mother? My aunt? Which one was which? Was it me who was sorry?

All I knew before that moment snapped away, and the deep hole of betrayal had no bottom. I plummeted alone.

It felt as if my lungs had gone flat, and I could

barely take breaths. Who was my father? My God, who was my father? In the distance, I heard myself wail, a drawn-out, savage sound.

I stayed locked in my bedroom for a week, even though it gave me no comfort. The curtains and matching dust ruffle had been custom-made from a print called Priority Rose. The once sweet pink flowers kept their disapproving, non-blinking, judgmental eyes on me. None of the books on the shelves wanted me near them. I wore only pajamas, and I wrapped a bed sheet around my shoulders when I got cold.

On day five, I had the vision, or hallucination, or whatever a shrink would call it. It wasn't a dream because I was wide awake, sitting on the side of my bed. She walked in, still wearing her funeral kimono. The mother I look like, not the mother who raised me or, at least, made an effort.

I thought she should have changed clothes, and then I looked down at my pajamas and bed sheet.

"It smells bad in here," she said.

"Maybe it's you." I resented her intrusion.

"Fresh air," she said. "You should get some fresh air. Take a drive."

"If it smells so bad, why don't you leave?"

She sat on the bed beside me. "So, what's on your mind, Miranda?"

"Please leave." More than the intrusion, I

resented her betrayal.

She stayed beside me until I finally said, "Aunt Loretta, what's with us Tillmans? Why. . . can't we love?" I'd come up with the idea while in my self-imposed exile. "Do you think it's genetic?"

"People love in different ways. Some people give it, but I preferred to receive it."

"I can't believe you'd say that."

"It's who I am."

"Is *preferring* not to give love the reason you gave me away or never got married?"

"Well, it seems that in the wardrobe of life, independence fit me better." She looked around. "What's going on with these curtains? They're so judgmental."

"Didn't you ever dream of raising me as your daughter?"

She fiddled with her obi. "Miranda, I believe dreams travel their own highways. Some get stuck in the slow lane or in the back of the line at a stoplight. You have to trust that they'll eventually show up, and when they do, it's time to go on an adventure with them."

"That's it? I ask if you ever dreamt of raising me and you talk about stoplights. You give some excuse about stoplights and slow lanes? How about alien abductions or some other ridiculous gobbledygook?"

"I don't give excuses if that's what you want."

"You don't give anything. You run away from everything."

"I also ran *toward* things."

"I'm afraid, Aunt Loretta."

"What are you afraid of?"

"What if I turn out like you?"

"You could do worse."

There was a tap on my bedroom door. Aunt Loretta vanished. I got up, turned the knob, and the housekeeper held out a tray of freshly baked chocolate chip cookies.

"I'm not hungry," I said and shut the door. "Go away."

Doctor Avery gave me a stern look when I said, "My mother, my aunt mother, came to see me." Because of that look, I didn't expand any further about the episode, Aunt Loretta, or anything else. In the silence, I thought about love. I wondered if I had ever given it. And about self-pity, how it had crippled me. I thought about secrets, how huge some could be, and how different I am from my folks, and, like it or not, how similar I am to Aunt Loretta. Then, I thought about a lifetime of feeling caged and all the trips I had longed for. Aunt Loretta had said *I also ran toward things.*

We headed west, Fenry and me. First stop, Mr. Chows. I snapped open the fortune cookie and peeled out the strip of paper. It read, *Beware of cookies bearing fortunes*.

Our time on the road was filled with miles of wind stroking my hair through the open windows. Small pieces of my future were tossed up like a salad of dread and excitement, and tremendous freedom.

He forced me to go slow, to discover the lessons of the back roads, and he taught me the rewards of unpredictability. I had a fistful of empty postcards in the glove compartment, and my own duffels on the back seat. We stopped in Cawker, Kansas to admire the largest ball of twine, and I mailed a snapshot to my parents, the ones who raised me.

ACKNOWLEDGMENTS:

Much gratitude for the support and wisdom of all of you who endured the tedious process that shaped this collection. Whether editing issues, or content, you had my back. Penelope James, Mike Irby, Laurie Richards, Shawna Goodrich, Yvonne Nelson Perry, Lita Manson, Kendra Eskau, Zoe Ghahremani, and so many more.

For early support and encouragement, I am grateful to the Santa Barbara Writers Conference community, especially my pirate mentors John M. Daniel and John Reed, and a special nod to S.L. Stebel.

Much thanks to Vicki Abelson. Her monthly Women Who Write literary salon is this artist's equivalent of a creative stimulus package, or a spa day for her muse.

And, there is a special place in my heart for all the positive support and encouragement I received from my incredible friends and neighbors in The Terrace.